"A fun romp ~~through childhood.~~"
~BILL MYERS,
Creator of *McGee and Me*, Best-selling Author,
Award-winning Filmmaker

"I love it. My kids think *The Water Fight Professional* should be made into a movie!"
~JILL WILLIAMSON,
Award-winning Children's Author

"Reading *The Water Fight Professional* is more fun than licking a slug."
~JUDY COX, Children's Author

"The protagonist's offbeat profession and Angela Strong's vibrant voice make *The Water Fight Professional* a book that young teens will eat up. Want to keep energetic boys and girls entertained for a few hours? Hand them this book."
~JEANNIE ST. JOHN TAYLOR,
Radio Host and Author/Illustrator of more than thirty books

THE WATER

FIGHT PROFESSIONAL

Written by
Angela Ruth Strong

Illustrated by
Jim Strong

Ashberry Lane

© 2014
Ashberry Lane
P.O. Box 665, Gaston, OR 97119
www.ashberrylane.com

Published in association with the literary agency of
Wordserve Literary Group, www.wordserveliterary.com

ISBN 978-0-9893967-8-3

Cover design by Miller Media Solutions
Illustrations by Jim Strong
Title font by Kimberly Geswein

FICTION / Middle Grade

To Jordan—
The *Real* Water Fight Professional

I have fought the good fight …
2 Timothy 4:7

Chapter One:

Splish, Splash, Water Fight and a Bath

Crouching behind a scratchy bush, I balanced a squishy water balloon in each hand.

Austin Clairmont's family slowly walked down the brick path of the nature trail. Very slowly. Was his mom really reading all the little signs that described each plant? People only read those on field trips.

My right foot tingled like it was starting to fall asleep.

The family turned left to go over the footbridge. I awaited my victim on the wrong path. This wasn't part of the business plan.

The Clairmonts strolled out of my line of vision—even Austin's super-tall dad who hired me to soak Austin in the first place. He'd paid me to use two water balloons and my Mega Drench 200, the water gun tucked in my belt behind my back. It was my only sale on that cloudy, early summer day.

Lucky for me, unlike my own dad, Mr. Clairmont liked to spend money. He'd come right up to my booth in the park and arranged for my services. Of course, since Austin was a whole year older than me and going into 8th grade at Cole Valley Christian School, I would have to be sneaky in my attack or he would certainly get me back.

Half crawling, half running, I started after the family. My sneakers kept my bridge crossing silent. I slowed down as I came to the bend and peeked around the corner.

Perfect. Austin had gone down the hill next to the fish-viewing windows.

I crept backward two steps to the railroad tie stairs which led up to an overlook of the pond, waterfall, and windows. I couldn't have planned it better.

Mr. Clairmont caught my eye through the tree branches and winked.

My pulse picked up.

I angled my body so there was a clear shot through the tree branches. Lifting the red balloon in my right hand, I focused on my target and counted down in my head. Three … two … one … FIRE!

Splat. Direct hit.

"What?" Austin leaped off the bench he was standing on and examined his royal blue T-shirt, now a navy color where the water had hit him.

The Water Fight Professional

Austin's two brothers laughed and looked around, but they didn't spot my second balloon before it arrived. Yikes. I hit Austin's little brother. That meant trouble, but I had to finish the job.

I pulled the Mega Drench out from under my belt and charged down the steps with a war cry. My position had been perfect for launching water balloons, but if I stayed there, the brothers would find me for sure, and I would have no escape. "Wah!" I yelled, gun pointed in front of me as I turned the corner.

One run-by soaking coming up.

Austin saw me. "It's Joey," he yelled.

"Who's Joey?" asked the little brother.

I aimed the nozzle slightly to the left of Austin—the Mega Drench never shot straight—and pulled the trigger.

"He's the professional water fighter." Austin jumped behind his big brother, Grant, to avoid my attack.

I doused the fifteen-year-old. Crud.

"Hey," yelled Grant. "You're gonna regret this."

I was already starting to, but that was the hazard of my chosen career. Mr. Clairmont high-fived me as I kept moving down the path, heart pounding in my ears.

He was the only one still laughing.

3

I glanced over my shoulder.

Austin had his mom's water bottle in hand and was in hot pursuit.

I faced forward and ran faster.

Heavier footsteps scuffed past Austin's. Grant was gaining on me.

Glancing back, I extended my gun and shot as I ran.

Water dripped from Grant's chin, but that didn't stop him.

How was I going to escape?

"Get him," shouted Austin. His voice faded behind me. I must have worn him out.

Sliding on gravel, I tried to leap toward a second bridge, but Grant grabbed my shirt. My collar held me back like a dog on a leash. I twisted side to side, whipping him back and forth, and jerked him off balance.

Grant tumbled to the ground but wrapped an arm around my ankle on the way down.

I lost my footing and joined him on the hard wooden planks.

Austin reappeared. I hadn't worn him out. He'd just ducked down to the creek to fill up the water bottle with slimy green stuff. Sick. That was so much worse than the drinking fountain water I used in my balloons.

4

I kicked at Grant and clawed at the bridge. No use.

Austin stepped forward with a huge grin on his face.

I shielded my head with my arms as algae and duck poop greased my body. My water gun bumped against my shoulder.

Oh, yeah. I was still armed.

Rolling onto my back, I aimed the weapon to the side of my assailants and fired. Woohoo!

"No way." Austin reached down for my right arm and Grant grabbed my left.

I tried to pull the brothers together so they would hit heads, but that must only work in kung fu movies.

Austin hauled me toward the side of the bridge. He wouldn't—

"Let me go," I hollered.

"I'd rather lick a slug." Austin didn't even break stride.

Grant paused, but didn't relax his grip on my arm. "Didn't you lick a slug on our camping trip last year?" he asked Austin.

"Oh, yeah."

"Ready?" asked Grant.

"Set," answered Austin.

"Go," they yelled together and tossed me over the railing.

5

I flailed through the air, barely catching my breath before splashing into the icy, murky pond.

A fish slipped past my neck.

I emerged to the sounds of laughter.

Baby Clairmont—I didn't know his name—had caught up with his brothers and they all smirked down at me from the bridge. Mr. Clairmont's tall frame doubled over in laughter in the distance. He was the reason I was floating in the muck. Was it worth it?

I thought of the soggy dollar bills stuffed into my jeans pocket. Oh yeah. It was worth it. I would do it again every day that summer if I got the chance.

Chapter Two:
A Delicious Bet

I shivered in the breeze then shook like a dog to dry off. Trudging back up the hill toward the park, I headed to my water fighting booth. Business was done for the day. I deserved a hot shower. I deserved dry clothes. I deserved—

A merry melody rang through the air.

Yes. I deserved ice cream.

After stuffing water balloons, a water gun, and a "Water Fighter" sign into my green camouflage backpack, I flagged down the ice cream truck.

"How's business going?" asked Dan, the college student behind the wheel. Dan, Dan, the Ice Cream Man had been driving the ice cream truck since the summer I turned eight. Next year he would graduate from Idaho's own Boise State University.

"Look at me." I groaned.

Dan surveyed me from my damp cap to soggy socks. "Tough job?"

"My only job." I focused my attention on the

ice cream prices. "I don't even have enough to buy an out-of-this-world triple dip today."

"Yeah, this weather isn't doing me any favors either." Dan frowned at the gray sky before focusing back on me. "Hey, aren't you freezing? Why do you want ice cream?"

"I'll take a fudge pop." I dug into my pocket for a dollar ninety-eight. "If I don't spend this money before I get home, my dad will make me put it into a savings account and I won't see it again until I'm your age. And worse, my mom never buys me ice cream."

"Never?" Dan pulled my treat from his freezer.

"Never," I answered solemnly.

"Then I guess I'll be seeing a lot of you this summer." He shifted back to drive.

"As usual." I saluted as the truck and its tunes faded into the distance. After ripping the paper off the fudge pop, I licked the ice cream. My tongue stung from the freezing temperature, and goose bumps popped up on my arms. But as cold as I was, I didn't rush home. I had to finish eating every speck of chocolaty goodness before my mom saw me. Our townhouse was located directly across the street from the park, so I circled the block to kill time. Turning right at the corner, I ran into my best friend and his lawn mower. "Hi, Chance."

Chance Zabransky wiped sweat from his forehead. He obviously wasn't as cold as I was. "Hey. I just made twenty bucks in two hours."

I only had two cents jingling in my pocket. "That's not bad."

"How much did you make today?" Chance was all about competition.

I guess when you've won every single sport you've played, it would become a habit. "Not that much." I shrugged and started walking faster.

Chance pushed the mower beside me. It didn't take any extra effort for him to keep up. His legs were longer than mine.

We used to be the same height. That was when he was known as "Fat Chance." Then during 6th grade he grew. And grew. And grew. Now people called him "Zabransky" as if he should be compared to Jordan and Gretzky. I kinda missed Fat Chance.

"Maybe you should mow lawns," he said.

Never. First of all, I hated mowing lawns. Second, I was sure I could never mow a lawn as

9

well as Chance did.

"I can make a lot of money as a professional water fighter." My tongue was numb, but I kept licking the fudge pop.

"How long were you at the park today?"

"I don't know. I don't wear a watch." Yes, I sounded a little babyish.

We turned around a second corner. There was Chance's house with the basketball key painted on the driveway.

"Well, do you think you made ten dollars an hour like I did?" he asked.

"No," I pouted. *Go home, Zabransky.*

Chance laughed. "I bet you couldn't."

"I bet I could." Of course I could. It would just have to be a sunny day.

"I'll give you a month to average over ten dollars an hour."

I took a deep bite of my fudge pop. Brain freeze. "Starting tomorrow." Whoa. That was more like a brain fart. There was no way I could average the kind of money he was talking about.

Chance grinned like the Cheshire Cat. "Awesome. You have until the Fourth of July, then."

The ice cream curdled in my stomach. I was a water fighter because it was fun. Chance had just sucked the fun right out of it.

"What are we betting?" Chance crossed his arms.

Too late to back out now. I straightened up. Because even if Dad said I should never make bets, I was going to win. But … what would I want to win? "The winner gets an out-of-this-world triple dip ice cream cone."

"That's a start." Chance bit his lip and squinted. Sometimes he seemed more bully than buddy. "The loser should have to do something awful."

I thought back to the brothers on the bridge. "The loser has to lick a slug."

"Oh, I've already done that. Haven't you?"

"Um …" I couldn't admit I'd never licked a slug before.

My annoying neighbor, Isabelle Lancaster, came walking her dog on the opposite side of the street. Her dog was actually pretty cool. He looked like a bear and he was great fun to wrestle with. It bugged the boogers out of me that Prissy Izzy owned such an awesome animal.

"The loser has to kiss Isabelle's dog." Yet

11

Isabelle kind of looked like a dog herself, her long pigtails swishing around like Cocker Spaniel ears. "No, worse."

Chance actually cackled like a witch. "What could be worse?"

"The loser has to kiss Isabelle." Ew ... now licking a slug sounded delicious.

Chance shook his head. "That's not so bad."

I felt as if I'd been hit by a water balloon in the chest. "Are you serious?"

"Whoa." Chance held up a hand. "If you're afraid to kiss a girl, then that's exactly what we'll bet—since you're gonna lose anyway."

I had to win now. As I started for home, I said, "Fat chance."

Chapter Three:
Barf-O-Bits

I hadn't meant to sound as if I were calling Chance fat. He wasn't fat anymore. But he still gave me a dirty look from behind his lawnmower as he stomped toward the garage. The truth was I missed the kid he used to be. I mean, kissing girls? Last summer we both would have gagged at the idea.

I knew about girls. I had a little sister. Girls talked a lot. They giggled for no reason. And they cried if you threw a water balloon at them.

It's weird. It's irritating. It's weirditating.

I'll still get married someday. Probably to a circus performer. I mean, have you ever seen what can be done on a flying trapeze? The girls who flipped through the air were nothing like my sister or Isabelle. They're daring. They're brave. And they wouldn't cry if you threw a water balloon at them.

I tossed my Popsicle stick in the garbage can by the side of our house, grabbed the mail from the mailbox, and ran my tongue along my lips to destroy any evidence before going inside. Mom couldn't think I had "ruined my appetite." She refused to believe that the reason I didn't eat her ground turkey rolls or salmon quiche was because they're nasty.

My sister, Christine, sat backward on her knees on the couch with her nose to the window.

"What are you doing?" I don't know why I asked. I never understood her anyway.

"I'm waiting for Parker." She didn't even look up.

"Who's Parker?"

"He's the mailman. He's cute."

I rolled my eyes. Last year she thought Dan, Dan, the Ice Cream Man was cute. And she's only nine. Boys were so different from girls. "The mail already came." I dropped a pile of envelopes on the table.

My mom spun into the room. Her hair was long and slick like a Slip 'N Slide, and when she spun it looked like one of those brushes at the car wash. She grabbed her foot in one hand mid-spin and extended her leg up by her head in a stretch that would make me cry "uncle."

14

That might seem strange to most kids, but it was pretty normal around here.

"The mailman came twice yesterday." Mom balanced on her other leg. "And Parker is cute."

"He sounds crazy."

Christine turned her head at that. "He's not crazy. He's just new. Delivering mail is a hard job."

Mom swung her leg from the front of her body to her back and leaned forward, picking up the pile of mail from the table. She dropped into the splits. "Delivering mail *must* be hard. Parker delivered the Lancaster's mail to us. Joey, take this over to Isabelle's house, please."

"No way." I would rather eat salmon quiche than have to deal with Prissy Izzy.

Christine jumped off the couch. "I will, Mommy."

Christine thought Isabelle was a princess or something. And all the girls at my school thought Christine was an angel. Even worse, they all wanted to grow up to be my mom—a dancer/actress/singer. Where were all the girls who dreamed of becoming trapeze artists?

"Thank you, sweetie." Mom cha-cha'd back to the kitchen.

15

I followed, even though I greatly feared whatever she had fixed for dinner. "Mom, do you think if the mailman delivered Isabelle's mail to us that he might accidentally deliver our mail to them?"

Mom swayed side to side as she loaded the dishwasher. "Maybe."

"Noo …" I wailed.

Nothing fazed my mom. Though she was talking to me, I know she was imagining herself on stage. "I'm sure the Lancasters would bring any of our mail over to us if they got it—just like we're doing for them."

"But … but … my Galactic Turbo Drench 3000. And my water balloon slingshot." Dad had helped me order them last week—after I gave two dollars of tithe at church.

"Don't worry, honey." Mom did a body roll.

Now *that* was strange.

I would have to meet this Parker character—let him know I was expecting a package.

Problem solved. Deep breath.

"I ran into Chance's mother at the supermarket today. She told me about the golf camp Chance is going to. I signed you up."

Why did Mom have to create an even bigger problem?

Golf: The world's most boring sport. (According to me.)

Me: An easily distracted bundle of energy. (According to Mrs. Lyons, my 6th grade teacher.)

What could my mom have been thinking? "I don't want to play golf." Especially with Chance.

Mom wiped the counter and pulled a bowl out of the fridge.

Had she heard me?

After a moment she glanced up. "It will be good for you. You're not doing anything else this summer."

My mouth opened. No words came out. Maybe I didn't sign up for all kinds of sports the way Chance did, but I kept pretty entertained. I certainly didn't sit around watching TV and surfing the Internet all day like some kids.

No, I was a businessman.

"Mom, I've got to run my business. I've got to earn ten dollars an hour. I've got to …" I made the mistake of looking in the bowl Mom put on the counter. "I've got to barf." The lumpy red chunks in a saliva-looking goo made my stomach

17

churn. "Mom, did you throw up?"

Mom kissed my head. "That's your dinner."

I slouched onto a barstool.

Golf + vomit soup = Mom destroying my vacation.

She sashayed past me, not even noticing the fact that I was doubled over as if I'd been punched in the gut. In the summer, Mom performed at the Starlight Mountain Theatre. She went to rehearsal almost every night.

As if timed to the second, my dad returned home from work and Mom swung her dance bag over her shoulder. He spun her around twice then twirled her out the door before turning to me. "Hey, Joe."

Dad was the only one who called me Joe instead of Joey. It made me feel like a man—though it wasn't quite as strong a name as "Zabransky." I sat up straighter. "Mom made barf-o-bits for dinner."

Dad chuckled as he headed toward the kitchen. "It can't be that bad." He looked into the bowl. "Gazpacho!"

My eyes grew wide. "What did you say?"

Dad pushed the bowl away. "It's … it's … a

bad word," he muttered. "Your mom knows I hate it."

I zoned out. Gazpacho was a bad word? I'd never heard it before. But I liked the sound of it.

"Come on." Dad headed back out the way he'd come. "We're going to McDonald's."

Woohoo. Dad would give Christine and me a small amount of money, and we would have to decide what we were going to buy for dinner. It was never enough to buy everything we wanted, but it sure beat a bowl of barf.

Dad gave us a budget whenever we went anywhere to teach us a financial lesson. It was his excuse for taking us to the circus, the movie theater, or the arcade.

Ah-ha! My dad's thriftiness and business sense could be just the weapon I needed to win the bet with Chance—a secret weapon, because I couldn't tell Dad about the bet. He once read me some scriptures on how foolish gambling was.

If he found out I'd made a bet, I would be in some deep gazpacho.

Chapter Four:

Pedal Power

"Do you want to go to the zoo with us, Joey?" Mom called up the stairs.

I stretched the neck of another balloon to fit around the bathroom faucet and turned the spigot. "I've got work to do, Mom," I yelled back.

"Work?"

I sighed as I twisted the water balloon into a knot. "Water fighting, remember? Dad gave me a new idea for my business."

"Oh." Mom stopped talking, but I didn't hear any footsteps carrying her away. "Well, you could come to Julia Davis Park with us. We're going to rent a paddle boat too."

The zoo was in Julia Davis Park. But even cooler was the lagoon filled with ducks and paddle boats. The paddle boats were fun—especially if you used them like bumper boats.

I stuffed balloons in my backpack and slung it over my shoulder. Maybe I could set up business at Julia Davis for the day. I galloped down the stairs and collided with Mom. "Okay."

Mom put her arm around me and ushered me out the door. Her gaze shifted to the clouds. She was already back in cha-cha land.

I looked up too.

The clouds were little and fluffy. The sun was burning and blinding. Perfect for my profession.

I pulled the door of Mom's lime-green hybrid open, tossed my backpack on the floor mat, and plopped into the front seat.

"Ew ..." a familiar voice groaned from behind me. "You didn't tell me your gross brother was coming."

I spun around.

Prissy Izzy.

"Ew ..." I mimicked. "You didn't tell me the annoying neighbor was coming."

Christine ignored me. "I didn't know Joey was coming," she said to Isabelle.

The driver's side door clicked open and Mom climbed in.

"Mom," Christine whined. "Why does Joey have to come?"

Isabelle answered, "He *does* belong in the zoo."

I held one arm overhead and scratched my arm

21

pit like a monkey. "Ooh-ooh, eee-eee."

Mom started the ignition. "Joey isn't going to the zoo with us. He's water fighting at Julia Davis today."

Christine sat back and crossed her arms. "Good."

♦ ♦ ♦

Business *was* good. My dad suggested that when nobody wanted to hire me, I should offer my services for free. That way the person who got wet would pay me to retaliate. Retaliation was fun.

I stuffed a wad of dollar bills in my pocket. Yeah, it was a wad. In two hours I had made twelve dollars. It wasn't enough to beat Chance, but I was getting closer.

A middle schooler in a visor walked by.

"Hey, kid!" I called from my picnic table.

He looked my way. "Me?"

"Yeah." I motioned him over. "I'm a professional water fighter. Business is slow, so I'll make you an offer. You pick the person, and I'll throw two water balloons at him free of charge."

The kid laughed. "Free of charge? I'll go for that." He pointed toward the bridge that crossed

22

over the creek leading to the lagoon. It led from the park to the Discovery Center, a really cool science museum with a robot display for the summer. "That's my mom in the yellow T-shirt."

I squinted.

The woman in yellow had short blonde hair and a pointy nose.

"She kind of looks like my old teacher," I said.

The boy smiled. "Mrs. Lyons?"

"Yes." Oh no.

"Soak her."

My throat made a weird, croaking noise. "I can't throw water balloons at a teacher."

"Why not?" Mrs. Lyons's son laughed. "She can't send you to the principal's office anymore."

I took a deep breath, but shook as if I had just guzzled an energy drink. "All right."

Mrs. Lyons strolled closer.

I scanned the area for a hiding place. Maybe she wouldn't know it was me who bombed her. But that defeated the whole purpose of offering my services for free. I wanted her to hire me to get her son back. Without another thought, I rushed toward the bridge and ducked behind a tree. "Please let Mrs. Lyons forgive me," I whispered to

23

God.

The wooden planks on the bridge creaked, then flip-flops slapped on cement. This was it.

"I'm sorry, Mrs. Lyons," I yelled as I leaped to the pathway from my hiding spot. As if it were a reflex, my arms cocked back one at a time and hurled the weapons.

Mrs. Lyons jumped and let out a short scream as the balloons burst, one against her shoulder and the other against her hip. "Oh, my. Oh, my. Joey?"

"Hi, Mrs. Lyons."

"What ... what was that for?"

"Umm ..."

Her son rolled around on the grass behind me, laughing. Hey, I would probably be rolling too if it were my mom.

I grinned before I could stop myself. "I'm a water fight professional, Mrs. Lyons. Somebody you know wanted me to throw two balloons at you."

The kid jumped up. "I'll be on the paddle boats, Mom. Bye." He ran off.

"You can hire me to get him back." I grabbed another balloon and tossed it from hand to hand.

Mrs. Lyons's eyes narrowed. "How much do

you charge?"

Mrs. Lyons was a cool teacher. It was a bummer I wouldn't have her for 7th grade. "A cup of water costs fifty cents. A water balloon is seventy-five cents. And the water gun costs one dollar."

Mrs. Lyons dug in her purse. "Are there any discounts if I purchase multiple methods?"

I hadn't thought of that. It wasn't a bad idea.

"Here." Mrs. Lyons folded two dollars neatly into my hand. "I want you to drench Tristan."

I nodded. "Consider it done."

But the job was easier said than done. Tristan and his friend's boat floated on the lagoon out of reach.

I hurled a couple of balloons, but they fell short of the paddle boat and bobbed on the water.

Tristan picked them up and tossed them back at me. His arm was better than mine.

I ended up looking as if I'd gone for a swim. But if I shot from the water's edge … I pulled out my water gun and stepped forward.

Onto duck poop.

Nasty.

Okay, I would rent my own paddle boat and

chase him down. I ran across the playground to the rental booth.

Mom was there but didn't notice me. The clerk behind the counter must have asked about her Starlight performance. I could order a tiger's blood slushy right in front of her, and she wouldn't even hear.

"Mom, come on," Christine's voice called from behind me.

I turned around.

Christine and Isabelle waited in a paddle boat.

I charged across the patio and leaped onto the bench seat next to Christine, stuck my feet on the pedals, and shouted, "Go, go, go!"

Isabelle had the other set of pedals. "Where are we going?"

I leaned forward to see her around my little sis. "Mrs. Lyons hired me to soak her son. He's on a paddle boat."

"Tristan? All right." Isabelle started to pedal.

"Wait," Christine screeched. "Mom wanted to come with us."

I pedaled faster. "Mom's talking about the theater."

"Oh."

We didn't even go around the little island that started the journey to the lagoon. Instead, we spun the boat around and headed right down the skinny waterway lined with trees.

Watch out, Tristan.

Isabelle pedaled almost as fast as me. "Give me a balloon."

"No way."

Ducks swam in front of us.

"Stop!" screamed Christine.

"They'll move," said Isabelle.

We didn't stop.

The ducks got out of our way.

"Isabelle, if you pedal as hard as you can, I'll let you have a balloon."

"You're too kind." Isabelle didn't sound as if she meant it.

Christine whined some more. "I don't want to be in the middle of a water fight."

"Then get out."

Christine shoved me. "You get out."

I started to feel shaky again—this time with excitement, not fear. We floated under the bridge and entered the lagoon. Tristan was to our right.

We angled our boat toward his, and I kind of

turned my head away. Maybe he wouldn't notice me. I passed Isabelle a balloon and held the other behind my back. Our boat inched closer. "When I say three," I whispered.

Isabelle nodded. She looked as if she were trying not to smile.

"One … two …" I pulled the water balloon out from behind me. "THREE!"

Both of our balloons hit Tristan. They exploded and water ran down his skin.

"Hey," Tristan yelled.

Tristan's friend turned to look at me. "Let's knock him overboard."

"Eek!" Christine really panicked now.

"Retreat," I yelled.

Isabelle's feet spun faster.

I tried to keep up with her pace, but it was hard to do while pumping pressure into my water gun. I twisted in my seat and shot water across the lagoon.

It blasted Tristan's visor.

"You're gonna regret this!" Tristan yelled. "What gave you the idea that you could shoot me with your water gun?"

"Your mama," I yelled back.

Isabelle giggled.

Christine screamed. "Get out, Joey. I mean it."

"Good idea." I pointed toward the edge of the lagoon. "Let me climb out and the guys will leave you alone."

Christine practically twisted backward on the bench to watch the other boat. "They're gaining on us."

Isabelle and I stepped on the gas, but we were no match for the bigger boys.

Crash. Their boat slammed into ours.

The girls jerked toward me as our boat wobbled and floated a few feet away from our assailants.

Christine looked near tears. "Hurry," she whimpered.

Tristan aimed his boat as if to ram us again.

We were close to the bank, but we couldn't get there before the boys got to us.

I stopped pedaling.

"Joey," Christine shrieked.

"See ya," I stood up and dove Superman-style toward land. My hands hit the soft grass first. I pulled my legs forward so they wouldn't splash in the water. Then I rolled, log-like, away from the lagoon and ended up on my side, propped up by

29

one elbow.

Tristan stood up as if to follow me, but his buddy pulled him back down. They needed two guys to maneuver the boat.

I waved then fell back onto the grass. Mission accomplished.

Chapter Five:
Free as a Birdie

I stuffed my hands in my pockets and kicked rocks around the front yard. Mom had told me to get ready for golf camp and wait for her by the car. I didn't have to do anything to get ready. What? Did she expect me to put on argyle socks and a sweater vest? Not happening.

The familiar hum of a mail jeep neared. The white vehicle raced down the street, then came to a screeching halt in front of our mailbox.

Crazy mailman. Oh, yeah, I needed to talk to him.

Parker looked to be about Dan, Dan, the Ice Cream Man's age. He had shaggy white-blond hair. A leather necklace with a pendant dangled in front of his wrinkled uniform. "Yo, dude," he called to me. "You live here?"

I lifted an eyebrow, nodded, and stepped closer so he could pass me a stack of envelopes and a dance catalog for my mom.

No big box holding a water gun.

"Thanks," I said. "Hey, I'm expecting a package soon." How could I say that I didn't trust him to deliver it to the right house?

"Cool." The guy's head bobbed up and down. "What's in the package?"

"I'm a professional water fighter, and I ordered a huge water gun and a water balloon slingshot for my business."

"Awesome." His head kept bobbing. "Why aren't you water fighting right now? It's a gorgeous day."

I made a face. "My mom signed me up for a stupid golf camp."

"Oh, dude. Golf isn't stupid. It's relaxing and challenging at the same time. Have you ever golfed before?"

I shrugged. "At my grandparents' cabin, my cousins and I take turns hitting pine cones at each other with golf clubs. That's kind of fun."

Parker laughed. "I'm sure your parents want the best for you, buddy. Take me, for example. I just wanted to be a surf instructor, but my parents insisted that I go to college. So I went. And that helped me get this job so I can save enough money to move to Hawaii."

Surfing would be fun. Mom used to call me a shopping cart surfer because I never sat down in the cart at the grocery store. "Well, you better get to work then."

"Oh, yeah." Parker blinked and looked out the windshield as if he'd just remembered where he was.

"Hi, Parker." My little sister ran down the sidewalk from the house. "Did you bring me anything?"

I rolled my eyes.

"Not this time, babe."

Christine clasped her hands together and tilted her head to the side with an overly sweet smile.

It made me feel sick—as if I'd eaten too much Halloween candy.

"Gotta go." Parker stuck his thumb and pinkie finger out and wiggled his hand in the hang loose sign. "Remember what I said, little dude."

"Sure." Whatever. "If you'll remember to bring me my package."

🌢 🌢 🌢

Chance had on argyle socks.

I trudged over to him in my flip flops, already

33

dreading the day.

Warm Springs Golf Course was on our edge of town next to Table Rock—a plateau with a cross on it that we hike up to every Easter. Older men putted around in golf carts. Little, little kids circled a large green with a hole in the middle. "Hi, ball," they said in unison. "Goodbye, ball." They swung.

I hoped to be half as good. I plopped down at a table on the patio under a striped umbrella. "Don't tell me we are going to have to talk to our golf balls. 'Hi, ball, what's your name?' Maybe I could draw a happy face on mine and pretend it's talking back."

Chance frowned. "That's just the Juniors class. We get to practice at the driving range, then play a game." Chance could probably teach the camp.

"Nice socks."

"Thanks," he said, as if I were giving him a compliment.

"All right, guys." A skinny man approached us, rubbing his hands together. "Are you excited?"

I was pretty sure he was excited enough for all of us.

He pointed to a bin of golf clubs. "Find a driver in your size, then follow me."

Chance had his own clubs, so I trailed after some other boys to the bin. I grabbed the first one by the fat part and swung it around like a sword. "En garde."

The others pretended not to see me.

What boring heads.

Chance stepped in front of me and pulled out another club. "This one is your size, Joey."

"Thanks, Zabransky," I muttered as we joined the boring heads at the driving range.

Mr. Enthusiasm demonstrated the proper swing technique then had us give it a whirl.

I was the only one who actually whirled.

"Joey, Joey, Joey."

"What, what, what?"

The guy stepped behind me and adjusted my grip. He pushed my shoulders down and had me swing the club like the pendulum on a clock for a moment. "Can you keep this arm straight and bend the other one at the same time?"

"I can pat my head and rub my tummy at the same time."

"Great." He acted excited for me, but left to help someone else as if I were hopeless.

"Just great." I took a deep breath and tried it

35

again. I missed the ball.

Chance coached me from the next tee. "Keep your head down, Joey."

Head down. Arm straight. Other arm bent. I pulled the club back like a baseball bat.

Whoosh—crack. The ball shot off to one side.

I grinned over my shoulder at Chance. Maybe I could do this after all.

Chance's club sliced through the air. *Ping.* His ball soared like one of my water balloons, landed out beyond anyone else's shot, and rolled even farther.

Mr. Enthusiasm was all over Chance then. "Beautiful. That was amazing. Can you do it again?"

Chance did it again and again and again until we finally got to head out on the course.

I flexed my fingers and rolled my head from side to side. I pulled my shoulders back and began to jog.

"Joey, where's the fire?" Mr. Enthusiasm laughed at his own joke.

I didn't see why it was funny. "Let's go." I would have expected my eager instructor to race me to the tee.

"Golf is a game to be enjoyed." He demonstrated his definition of enjoyment by walking even slower.

I blinked and shook my head. Golf was a game for snails.

Chance patted me on the back. "Take your time. Do it right."

Take your time? That's what time outs were invented for. Where was the adrenalin rush? The energy? What a waste of a sunny day.

For the first half of the course, I felt as if I were Chance's caddy. I hit a few balls. And I knocked the boring heads' balls into the rough when nobody was looking. Then I just stared up at the trees and imagined how I might climb them if I were going to ambush the golfers with a sneak water gun attack. Now that would be an enjoyable game.

"Joey," Chance called.

I jolted back to reality.

Chance and I were the only ones left on the green.

"Where did everyone else go?" Dare I hope the torture was over?

Chance pointed across a cement pathway.

37

"They're on the next hole. I came back to find you. Come on." Chance trotted away.

"Oh, no, Chance. You can't run. 'Golf is a game to be enjoyed.'" I mimicked our instructor.

Chance's mouth dropped open as if he was shocked. "Aren't you having a good time?"

I sighed. "This sport is so slow. We need a golf cart or something."

"We get to ride in a golf cart on the last day … Joey? Joey!"

I'd already taken off toward the parking lot for golf carts by the clubhouse. The course curved its way back around so the hole we just finished was next to where we had started.

Chance easily kept up with me. "Joey, you can't take a golf cart."

"Do they leave the keys in these things?" I climbed behind the wheel. I bet I'd make a great race car driver someday.

"I hope not," Chance said, but he looked kind of curious.

The key was sitting on the dash, an open invitation to me to use it.

"Wouldn't you love to ride in one of these?" I tempted him, jingling the key in front of him. "I'll drive. There's no other way we can catch up with our group, and we don't want them to worry about us." I exaggerated a little, but hey, it was for the benefit of my team. *Do to others as you would have them do to you*, right?

Chance hesitated, but smiled. "I guess if you're driving, then I can't really get in trouble."

"What could they do?" I looked around to make sure we were alone. "Kick me off the course?"

"They could."

"Perfect." I turned the key in the ignition. My stomach fluttered as the engine sputtered to life. I tested the accelerator pedal.

We jerked a few feet. It was much easier than a paddle boat.

"Woohoo," I hollered.

Chance laughed.

I gripped my fingers around the steering wheel and stepped down hard on the accelerator.

We shot forward. Chance grabbed onto the side of the vehicle for safety.

"That's right. Hang on," I yelled as the golf cart swerved side to side down the path. I drove better than Parker the Postman.

"I can't believe we're doing this," Chance shouted at me.

We rounded a corner at what might be considered illegal speed. Wind pushed against my hair and chilled my sweaty forehead. I was as free as a bird—or maybe a birdie, since we were playing golf.

"We have to stop." Chance must have had a sudden attack of conscience, though sometimes I felt he cared more about what people thought than what God thought.

"No way." If God wanted me to stop, He would have to send a talking donkey.

Chance pointed past my face. "Our instructor wants us to stop."

I turned my head to see Mr. Enthusiasm looking more like Mr. Unenthusiastic. I couldn't hear what he was saying, but he waved his arms as he ran after us. Not quite a talking donkey, but I guess it would have to do.

I planned to slow down, really I did. But once I faced forward, I discovered that we'd run out of pathway. There was no chance for me to hit the brakes.

The little vehicle careened into the grass.

Chance and I vibrated along the turf for a moment, but not for long. We hit a slight incline and sailed into a sand trap as if the cart thought it were one of my golf balls.

Chapter Six:
Slip Slidin' on Waves

Chance didn't get kicked out of golf camp. He was right about me being the one to get in trouble. And it helped that his dad had a membership to Warm Springs Golf Course.

My dad didn't.

No, my dad was more than a little upset that Mom paid for my registration, and I wasn't even allowed to attend. I spent the rest of the week grounded. The most I could do was look out the window. It made golf seem exciting.

Finally Saturday came. Freedom. My parents originally said I was grounded until Sunday, but I think they got sick of me. I hauled my backpack out from under my bed. Time to get down to business.

My cell phone played the soundtrack from *Pirates of the Caribbean*. Chance.

I clicked the answer button, though now that I could talk on the phone I had nothing to say. And I really didn't want to hear about golf. I sighed.

"Hello?"

"Hey, Lightning Michaels. Everybody was talking about you at camp. I'm like a celebrity just because I flew into the sand trap with you."

"Really?" Cool. I had a nickname and everything.

"It was awesome. And my parents aren't mad at you at all. My mom says it's her fault because she was the one who suggested you try it."

I frowned. "What's that mean?"

"Oh, just that she should have expected your hijinks. That's what she called it—hijinks."

My nickname didn't seem as cool anymore. Chance was expected to be the next Tiger Woods, and I was expected to get into trouble.

"But anyway, I'm calling to see if you want to go to Roaring Springs with us."

I dropped my backpack. "Yeah."

Dad only takes us to the water park once a summer—whenever he can get the biggest discount.

"Don't you need to ask your parents?"

Unfortunately. "I'll call you back." I leaped down the stairs, praying that my parents would let me go. I had learned my lesson. No more hijinks.

43

Dad sat at his desk, balancing the checkbook—his favorite pastime.

"Can I go to Roaring Springs with Chance?"

Dad didn't even look at me. "How much money do you have?"

"I made twelve bucks last week."

Dad's head snapped up. "Why didn't I know this? Where is it? Did you tithe?"

There are pictures in Mom's scrapbooks from my second birthday party when Dad gave me my first piggy bank. It was divided into three sections—one for church, one for the bank, and one for the store. Ever since I can remember I was supposed to divide my money up as soon as I got it.

Each month my dad would take all the money from the bank portion to deposit it into my savings account.

The rest was up to me.

I bit my lip. "It's still in my pants pocket."

Dad shook his head as if he were shocked by such irresponsibility. "Did it go through the wash?"

I nodded.

Dad set his pen down and leaned back.

I should have asked Mom.

"Even if you don't tithe or put any of your money in savings, you still don't have enough to pay for Roaring Springs."

I groaned and collapsed into a chair. "Most parents pay for their kids to do things."

"And that is one of the reasons our society accumulates so much debt."

I have this theory that when my parents die I will inherit millions. My dad stuffs money in the bank like gerbils stuff food in their cheeks. Until then, we will live "with a budget."

But maybe Dad was onto something with all his debt talk.

"So ... if you want me to learn about the dangers of debt, you should give me a loan." I held my breath.

Dad crossed his arms. "What are you suggesting?"

"You—" I paused for emphasis "—loan me ten dollars, and I will pay you back eleven before the end of the month."

Dad narrowed his eyes. "If you don't, interest goes up. It will cost you an extra dollar for every week your payment is late."

45

I jumped up. "I promise."

Dad yelled after me as I ran for my phone. "This is a one-time offer!"

Fine. I only needed one full day of play. Then I would be back at my water-fighting business earning enough money to repay my parents—and more than enough to win the bet with Chance.

◆ ◆ ◆

The Avalanche.

My heart pummeled my ribcage as Chance and I sat facing each other in the raft.

The lifeguard pushed us over the side of the ride shaped like a half pipe.

We slid straight down.

It was impossible not to scream. It was like floating over the side of a waterfall, but at the last moment, instead of drowning, we slid back up the other side of the huge wall.

I laughed for a moment then tried to talk over the sound of my pulse. "Let's go ride that new slide—the one where the trap door opens under your feet."

"Yeah."

Chance and I knocked knuckles.

We ran past Double Trouble, the waterslide that drops you in midair, and crossed the bridge over The Endless River. We were almost to The Corkscrew when we ran into the Clairmonts. I still owed them one for dumping me in the trout pond.

"Hi, Austin. Hi, Grant." Chance didn't say anything to Baby Clairmont. Apparently neither of us knew the kid's name.

"Hey, Zabransky." Austin looked over at me. "You ready for another swim, Joey?"

"Very funny." I kept walking. "We're headed to The Corkscrew. See you later."

Chance followed me and the Clairmonts followed Chance. Figured. We started up the massive winding stairway and made ourselves comfortable in line.

Baby Clairmont looked out over the parking lot. "I see our car."

The other boys turned to look. Big whoop.

We moved a couple of steps as the line shifted forward.

Grant pointed out over the water park. "Hey, there's Isabelle Lancaster and her friends. They're playing volleyball."

Austin twisted to get a better look. "Let's go

47

challenge them to a game after this."

"Okay," said Chance. The traitor.

"No way." I shook my head. "I took out a loan to come today. There's no way I'm going to spend my time playing in the sand."

Austin gave me a weird look. "It's *Isabelle*."

"I *know*." I talked to him like he was Baby Clairmont. "She's my annoying neighbor."

Grant laughed at me. "It won't be long before you're trying to kiss her."

Chance's eyes got big.

I gave him the I'll-punch-you-if-you-say-one-word-about-our-bet look.

Chance turned away. "Joey only likes circus girls," he said.

Whew. That was a close one.

Austin still laughed at me. "Circus girls are old. Come on. Just one game of volleyball."

Baby Clairmont piped up. "I'll go to the wave pool with you, Joey, if you don't want to play volleyball."

The wave pool did sound inviting, but I didn't want to spend my day with a baby. "That's okay."

The Corkscrew wasn't as fun as I expected it to be. But that was probably because I dreaded what

I had to do when the ride was over.

I guess I could forgive the Clairmonts. They didn't have any sisters and neither did Chance. Only I knew how prissy girls could be. Hmm … maybe I could show them. I told the guys I would meet them at the volleyball court and took off for my backpack.

When I got to the sand pit, all the boys were surrounding Isabelle. The other girls giggled and pointed from the side.

I rolled my eyes and unzipped my bag. "Hey, guys."

Chance looked over first. "No, Joey. Not today."

Austin glanced up—then did a double take. "You really want to start that again?"

I juggled two water balloons from hand to hand with a huge grin on my face.

The girls screamed and ducked for cover.

Except for Isabelle. She put one hand onto her hip.

Grant took two giant steps toward me and I thought about ducking for cover. "We're not here for a water fight," he growled.

"I know." Though a water fight would be fun.

49

"Haven't you ever played water balloon volleyball?"

Grant stopped. "No."

I instructed everyone to buddy up and grab opposite sides of beach towels. I made the girls get on one side of the net. We boys stood across from them. Chance had the other end of my towel. Baby Clairmont became the referee since numbers were uneven and he didn't have a buddy.

"If you get wet, you're out," I called. Now my friends would see how prissy girls really were. I plunked the first water balloon in the center of the towel I was holding. "Ready?"

Chance's gaze met mine and he gave a slight nod.

We bounced the balloon a couple times. One, two, three, fling.

The red balloon sailed over the net and headed for the sand on the other side.

I hoped it would burst all over Prissy Izzy.

Isabelle tugged hard on her towel, her partner, Mattea, stumbling after her. She dove to the ground and caught the balloon just in time.

"Yay," all the girls hollered.

I didn't even get a chance to boo.

50

Isabelle jumped to her feet and flung the balloon back our way.

Chance and I ran together as if we were in a three-legged race.

The balloon landed in the center of our towel.

Without a second thought, we pulled the towel tight and sent the balloon back across the net.

Isabelle could have caught the balloon, but Mattea didn't move fast enough. She tripped and landed in the sand and the balloon splattered all over her head.

"I'm the gazpacho," I yelled.

"Shut up, Joey. You're talking gibberish." Chance always focused completely on the game.

"Gazpacho is a bad word," I informed him. "I heard my dad use it the other day. I think it means vomit."

Chance translated my gibberish. "You're the vomit?"

I grinned. "Didn't you see the way I *threw up* that balloon?"

From there, Isabelle had to hold both sides of her towel by herself. I had to admit she wasn't bad. In fact, she was part of the remaining four. Chance and I still had our towel, and one other girl named

51

Nicole was on Isabelle's side. Isabelle and Nicole both had their own towels.

It wasn't really fair to have them competing against Chance and I, who shared only one. "You girls can downsize to one towel now."

Isabelle and Nicole stepped together.

"Wait," Baby Clairmont refereed. "One girl and one boy on each side."

"Aw …" I groaned. "Who put Baby Clairmont in charge?"

"You," Chance answered.

"Joey," Isabelle called my name. "You're on my side."

I kicked at the sand on my way under the net. I wouldn't look her in the eye. "Why didn't you pick Chance?" I asked. "He's the athlete."

"Yeah," Isabelle said. "But you're the water balloon lover."

I shot her a death glare. "I am not."

Isabelle's cheek dimpled. "It's a compliment."

Chance yelled from across the net. "Ready?"

"Ready," Isabelle and I shouted in return.

Then, with confidence from Isabelle's belief in me, I contemplated the idea that Chance's strength might also be his weakness. I leaned forward to

52

whisper quickly before the game began. "Let's pop it to Nicole's side. Chance will trample her."

The balloon flew our direction.

We scrambled backward to catch it. Perfect.

Pop. We tossed it toward Nicole's side.

Chance rushed forward. He bumped directly into Nicole, who couldn't move as fast. Down they went. *Splat.* They both got soaked.

I won. I won! I beat Chance. That was a first. I celebrated the rest of the day by avoiding all girls—especially Isabelle.

Chapter Seven:

Two for Tuesday

I slipped my dollar-store water guns out of my pockets as if they were six-shooters, spun them around my fingers, and squirted one right into my mouth. Mmm … refreshing.

Chance had let me fill up my little water guns with clear Kool-Aid at his house. I didn't even know there was such a thing as clear Kool-Aid. Of course, I'd also been in 1st grade when I discovered that most moms didn't pack spinach leaves on peanut butter and jelly sandwiches.

Chance took a few practice swings with his baseball bat as I set up my business booth.

Grant, Austin, and Baby Clairmont joined us. They all had baseball mitts on their hands.

Chance pretended he was stepping up to the plate. "Pitch me one, Grant."

Grant looked around. "Where's the ball?"

Chance set the tip of his bat on the ground and leaned against it. "I thought you were bringing one."

I laughed. "I can pitch you a water balloon."

All heads swiveled my direction.

"Ah, yeah." Austin cheered.

"All right." Chance swung the bat up over his shoulder.

"It costs seventy-five cents." I was a businessman, after all.

Chance dropped his bat to the ground. "You've got to be kidding. That's more than two dollars for three pitches."

I thought back to Mrs. Lyons suggestion. I should make it sound as if I were giving them a bargain. "Actually, today is Tuesday, so if you buy two balloons, you get one free."

Grant dug into his pocket. "I'll do it." He handed me one dollar and two quarters.

Chance handed him the bat.

"Batter up," I said and picked up one of my balloons.

Grant stepped wide and raised the bat in the air.

"Here's the wind up," I commented like a sports announcer. "And the pitch." I tossed the balloon right in front of him. I never could have done that well with an actual baseball, but I'd had

55

a lot of practice with water balloons.

Grant leaned into his swing.

The bat made contact and the balloon exploded.

Water rained down on all of us.

"Woohoo," I hollered.

Grant got back into position.

More boys came running over. "Hey batter, batter," they chanted.

Grant sliced the air again, blasting another busted balloon high overhead.

This time younger kids came running.

"One more." I wound up like a professional pitcher, then sent the balloon sailing through the air.

Grant made contact and the balloon came flying directly back to me.

Before I had a chance to react, the balloon slammed into my stomach and blew up like dynamite. I fell backward, landing on my bum.

The crowd cheered.

"Hey," yelled Austin. "This is better than a dunk tank. I wanna try." Austin begged his brother for money and Grant gave in.

Other boys ran off, I assumed, to either go home and empty piggy banks or look for their parents to borrow cash. Yes, I could stand a little pain and wetness if it meant winning the bet with Chance.

Austin grabbed the bat from his brother.

A line of kids formed next to a weeping willow tree.

I counted five kids. At a dollar fifty a piece, including the Clairmonts, I would make over ten dollars an hour.

Chance slumped down at the picnic table. "You know you have to average the money you make today with all your other hours of water fighting," he reminded me. I don't think he was too worried about the bet. He just wanted his bat back.

57

"I know." I sounded like my bratty sister. I mentally calculated my earnings. Including the two previous hours, I had averaged seven dollars and fifty cents an hour. I was going to have to do better than that.

"Come on, guys." Chance groaned. "We're supposed to play ball. That's why I called you."

I frowned. "You didn't invite me to play baseball," I said over my shoulder as I pitched to Austin.

"Oh, yeah." Chance looked down. "Well, I thought you would be busy with your business."

I was busy with my business. Chance was the one sitting by himself. So why did I feel left out?

Austin's hit would have been considered a foul if we were on a baseball diamond.

The kids behind him screamed as they got soaked.

Chance shrugged. "You can take turns playing right field with Baby Clairmont if you want."

That hurt worse than the balloon hitting my gut. Chance invited Baby Clairmont to play and not me? I pitched again.

It whizzed over Austin's head and landed in a bush. An umpire would have called it a ball.

"No fair," Austin shouted. "I shouldn't have to pay for that."

"O-kaaay." You gotta satisfy your customers. I grabbed two more balloons to toss. "I don't want to play baseball," I said to Chance. "It's almost as boring as golf."

"You're boring."

I dropped a balloon. It splattered on my shoes. How could Chance call me boring? I had kids lining up to play with me.

No ... I had kids lining up to *pay* me.

"Hurry up, Joey." Baby Clairmont bounced up and down.

I shook away bad feelings and pitched again.

The balloon burst on contact.

I didn't laugh along with everyone else. I just focused on Austin's last pitch. It was good.

A familiar-looking kid in a visor jogged over. Tristan Lyons.

Chance stood. "Did you bring a ball?"

Tristan held up a bat and ball. "Let's go."

Both boys strolled away. Grant and Austin took off as well, since their turns were over.

I studied the remaining kids in line.

They were all about Baby Clairmont's age.

59

I shrugged. What did it matter? I was making money.

After everyone had their turn, I finished collecting the cash and packed up for the day. I would return Chance's bat to him later. Trudging across the park, I counted out the money I needed to pay back my dad for most of the trip to Roaring Springs. It's not as if I would be using the money anytime soon, since nobody wanted to hang out with me. I paused when I reached the curb.

It wasn't a busy street, but Parker did tend to zip by awfully fast. His little white jeep rounded the corner toward me on two wheels.

At least I would have somebody to talk to.

The jeep pulled into the Lancaster's driveway and backed out facing the other direction. Parker raced away.

Or nobody to talk to.

I stepped out slowly into the street.

Parker was just being a crazy mailman. He probably needed a bathroom break.

But deep down it felt as if he didn't want to hang out with me either.

Chapter Eight:
King of the Wheelie

Gray, early-morning light made our living room look as if it belonged in an old black and white movie—the kind my mom always watched.

I usually didn't get up before the sun in the summertime, but I was dreading the day and just wanted to get it over with. My stomach twisted like one of the water slides at Roaring Springs. I sprawled on the couch and pulled my fleece Dallas Cowboys blanket over me.

I'm not into NFL football, but I have this fantasy of riding a bucking bronco or a bull. Whenever anybody asks me my favorite team, I always say the Cowboys. Seriously, who wanted to be called a Cheesehead or a Brown?

The blanket was a gift from Chance's mom last Christmas. She was the kind of mom who wore sports jerseys and yelled at the television whenever a game was on. Really, come to think of it, what did my mom and Chance's mom have to talk about?

Unfortunately, our moms had been talking a lot lately.

The front door thudded open and closed. Dad's running shoes squeaked on the hardwood floor.

Dad ran every morning—not because he cared about looking good, but because he thought it would keep him healthier and save him money on doctor's bills when he got older. He also had a weight bench in his bedroom. He was buff but balding—kind of like actor and fellow Idahoan Bruce Willis.

I popped my head up to talk to him over the back of the couch. "How could you let her do it, Dad?"

Dad's head swiveled my way. "What are you doing up, Joe?"

"I'm planning to run away."

Dad unscrewed his water bottle and leaned his hip close to my head on the other side of the couch. He took a gulp. "I don't think you have enough money to run away."

"I could join the circus."

"Not until you pay the fifty cents you still owe me."

"Argh." I groaned and dropped back to the

cushions. "Well, then I'm going to fake sick. Mom can't send me to tennis lessons with Chance if I throw up." The way my stomach churned, that would be easy enough to do.

Dad turned to climb the stairs. "Joe, you'll have to pay me back for every tennis lesson you don't go to. That's twelve dollars a week. You decide."

I kicked a throw pillow to the ground. "Thanks for the pep talk."

What in the world gave my mom the idea that I would enjoy tennis lessons? Tennis was a game of control. You had to keep a little ball within a few white lines. The sport should have died with the Pong video game.

Chance couldn't have agreed less. When Mom dropped me off at the tennis courts, he was bouncing back and forth, swinging his racket at an imaginary ball as zoned out as if he were wearing a virtual reality helmet.

"Hey, Chance," I mumbled.

Chance whipped around. "Joey. I didn't know you were coming."

I shrugged. "It wasn't my idea."

Chance shifted from foot to foot. "Have you played tennis before?"

"No."

Chance started to walk away. "Come on. I'll introduce you to our coach."

I trailed behind, my new tennis racket banging against my legs.

Other kids ran around. Most looked athletic like Chance. One scrawny kid stared back at me from behind bug-eyed glasses.

I sighed in relief. At least I could beat him.

"Joey, this is Coach Carpenter."

I expected a clone of our golf camp instructor, but looking up I saw no one. I looked down.

Coach Carpenter sat in a wheelchair.

My mouth opened, but no words came out.

"Hi, Joey," said Coach Carpenter.

"You play tennis?" was all I could think to ask.

Chance shoved me for being rude.

But I was starting to feel better. If this guy could play tennis sitting down, then I could certainly do it.

"Yeah, I play tennis." He smiled. Spinning one of the wheels on his chair, he turned sideways. "This is a specially designed wheelchair. My regular one is over there." He pointed toward the gate.

The wheelchair he sat in was certainly different.

64

The wheels were thicker and kind of angled out. They made me think of the difference between a road bike and a mountain bike.

I rode a mountain bike, of course. "Cool."

"Come here." Coach Carpenter rolled away.

I followed at a much slower pace. It might be kind of fun to ride in a wheelchair. I pictured myself careening down a hill. It would be like a constant soapbox derby.

Coach stopped at a short pole.

A tennis ball hung from it, connected by two small ropes that attached to the top and the bottom of the pole.

Coach had me pick up two plastic circle mats and place them on the ground where he pointed. "Stand with a foot on each circle."

I positioned myself at an angle to the pole.

Coach swung the ball around the pole. "It is going to unravel. I will tell you when to swing."

I thought back to my golf lessons. Head down, one elbow bent, the other straight, swing like a pendulum on a clock.

"Now."

My racket ripped through the air and hit the ball.

65

The tennis ball circled the pole like a tetherball.

Coach chuckled. "You've got energy."

I liked him.

He called the rest of the class over and discussed swings. Blah, blah, blah.

I just wanted to whack the ball again.

Coach went over the game rules and assigned us to nets.

I faced off with the scrawny kid.

He told me he'd never played tennis before either. Ha.

I hopped from one foot to the other, imitating Chance.

Scrawny Kid served.

I raced toward the ball and swung.

The ball sailed back over the net. Woohoo!

It went out of bounds. Boohoo.

Scrawny Kid served again.

I hit it.

It flew over the fence.

Over and over and over again I raced to the ball.

Over and over and over again the ball shot off in all directions.

Finally, when I got a good hit, Scrawny Kid

gracefully slammed the ball just out of my reach.

I wanted to smash my racket over his head. He must have lied about being new to tennis.

A whistle split the air.

We stepped forward and shook hands.

Scrawny Kid had a strong grip. "I play racquetball a lot," he said.

"Good for you," I said. I wanted to say: *I do cool things, too. I'm a professional water fighter.* But I didn't think he would care. I'd lost to him, and that was all that mattered.

Scrawny Kid moved up and I moved down. And that was as close as I got to being "king of the hill." Next, I was beaten by a girl. I'd like to say that I let her win, but no, I've never worked so hard in my life. In my defense, I didn't miss a single ball. In fact, I even hit a couple that I shouldn't have because they would have been out of bounds had I let them go.

Coach offered to help me at first but gave up when I didn't improve with his advice.

I'm sure my game was painful to watch—like when I beat Christine at air hockey because she constantly knocked the puck in on her own side. She scored almost all the points for me.

67

Chance and I never played each other. No, he was king of the hill. And I was what? Tennis court jester?

Coach whistled and rolled to a table with a water cooler.

I dropped my racket on the ground and jogged after him to get a drink. What I wouldn't do for a water gun filled with clear Kool-Aid. I gulped down the entire cup of water and wiped drops of sweat out of my eyes.

Chance joined me. "Good idea," he said and dumped his own cup of water on his head. He must have thought that I had dumped my cup on myself.

I chose not to explain that I was drenched in sweat.

"How's it going?" he asked.

"I haven't missed many balls," I said, refusing to announce that I'd been beaten by a girl. "I'm exhausted, though." I looked around for a bench or chair. The only chair I saw had wheels on it. Hmm …

"Yeah." Chance refilled his cup. "Just wait until we finish playing the second half."

I blinked. "We're only halfway done?" My body

suddenly felt twice as heavy. My Jell-O legs refused to hold me up any longer. "Do you think Coach will mind if I sit in his wheelchair for a moment?" Not waiting for a response I slumped into the seat.

Chance didn't answer, but he didn't move either. He just stared at me. His blank expression made me laugh.

"Oh, I wish I had one of these. It would be fun to roll down the stairs at home."

"Joey." Chance sounded like my mom when she's fed up.

I ignored him. "It's kind of like a bike without pedals. I wonder if I could pop a wheelie." I looked over the side of the chair at the wheels. It would take some balance.

"Get out, Joey."

"Hold on. I want to try this." I leaned forward then slammed back.

The wheelchair rocked a little.

I tried it again. Close.

"I don't think that's a good idea."

What did Chance know? He enjoyed stupid things like golf and baseball and tennis. I thought about Parker's mail jeep tipping sideways on two wheels when he turned a corner. Maybe I could do

69

that. Holding the large right wheel in place, I leaned toward it and spun the left wheel.

The wheelchair rose from the ground.

"We have liftoff," I announced, leaning farther out to keep the experiment from ending. Uh-oh, I leaned too far. Losing balance, the chair tipped more than I had intended.

My muscles tensed and my heart pounded as if I were three thousand feet above the ground rather than just three.

The wheelchair rocked backward with me still sitting in it.

Tim-ber.

I strained my neck to keep my head from hitting the cement, but nothing protected my back. I landed hard enough to put a dent in the tennis court—or so it felt. And then I couldn't feel anything. I couldn't even breathe. I heard a wheezing/croaking sound and realized it was me. "Eee ... eee ... eee ... eee." I couldn't stop.

It sounded like a dying cow.

Was I dying?

Floating heads surrounded me. Every eye focused on me.

"Eee ... eee ... eee ... eee." If I didn't die from a punctured lung, I would certainly die from embarrassment.

Some of the heads disappeared and Coach's wrinkled forehead filled the vacancy. "Joey? Can you move?" He sounded scared.

I couldn't even control my own voice box and he wanted me to move? Finally the wheezing stopped. I was so relieved that I just lay there for a moment, not sure if I could move my body or not. It was almost better not knowing. What if I actually did have to get my own wheelchair? It didn't seem like such a cool idea anymore. It made me feel sorry for Coach. But it also gave me more

71

respect for him.

"Nobody touch him." Coach grabbed Chance's arm. "My phone is on the table. Call 911."

I felt like crying. At first because of Coach's concern for me. Then because his fear scared me. I had no idea what consequences might come from my actions, but he did. That filled me with guilt.

I was a big idiot. My own stupidity made me want to cry even more. Then the throbbing pain started. I was sure my insides were mangled. I wrapped my arms over my face to keep my audience from seeing any tears that might slip out.

"He moved," shouted Scrawny Kid.

I moved? I hadn't even realized it until Scrawny Kid announced it. I wasn't paralyzed. Then suddenly I didn't care if he was scrawny anymore. He had a body that worked. And it was okay to be a "Fat Chance" or a "Baby Clairmont." They were healthy. They were whole. And maybe it wasn't that big a deal if I couldn't play sports as well as Chance. The important thing was that I could play.

Coach looked mad now. His eyes squinted at me from above. He was probably thinking about how I took all these things for granted. Who was I to gamble with my well-being and survive intact?

72

Why was Coach in the wheelchair? There was nothing fair about who was paralyzed and who was not.

"Get up," said Coach.

And though my chest hurt worse than a rumpload of bee stings, I got up.

Chapter Nine:

Hit Me with Your Best Slingshot

I balanced on the tree branch and wrapped my fingers around the rough rope.

The Clairmonts watched from the riverbank below.

I could do it. I knew I could. I squeezed the rope tighter, my heart pounded harder in my chest, and I took a deep breath. With a war cry, I jumped from my perch and swung through the air like Tarzan, except I had to do a little more than swing from tree to tree. I had to flip all the way over before landing in the river. I'd never done it before, but I told the Clairmonts I could, so there was no backing out.

The rope reached its peak faster than I expected.

Now or never.

Pulling my knees into my chest, I let the rope lift me up. I leaned backward and saw the water underneath me. I was upside down. All I had to do was finish the flip.

Tummy tight, I whipped my feet over my head and let go. Woohoo. I sailed down toward the river.

Splash. The icy water engulfed me. My lower right rib stung a little. I emerged, gulped air, and let the current carry me to solid ground. I waved to a couple of rafts floating by, then hiked back toward the rope swing.

My family may have had a townhouse and a tiny backyard, but with a park and a river just across the street, I wouldn't give up my little home in the Boise greenbelt for the biggest of mansions.

"All right." Grant gave me a pound on the back when I reached him.

I was pretty proud of myself actually.

Grant was a teenager and he couldn't even do what I did.

"That was some tricky gazpacho," said Austin.

I lifted my eyebrows. "Where did you learn that word?"

"Gazpacho?" Austin asked, but didn't wait for an answer. "It's a bad word. I heard Chance use it the other day." He shot me an evil grin.

From in the distance came the familiar melody of Dan, Dan, the Ice Cream Man's truck.

Grant grabbed his shoes. "Come on, guys. Let's go get ice cream."

I sat on the ground, holding my side. It throbbed. I fell back into the grass. "I can't. I don't have any money."

And I wouldn't have any money for a long

time. I owed Coach Carpenter fifty dollars for the handle I broke off his wheelchair.

Austin shook his head and water flew everywhere. "Well, why aren't you working today then?"

"Mom won't let me. I cracked a rib, remember? She wants me to take it easy."

Grant laughed. "But she let you go swimming?"

"No." I repositioned myself so I was sprawled completely in the sun. "I've got to stay here until my shorts dry so she won't find out." I wasn't being completely dishonest, was I? *It's not as if I'm telling any lies.* I pushed the guilt aside and tried to ignore God.

"Well, see ya around." Grant took off.

Austin got to his feet, too. "Bye, Joey."

Baby Clairmont moved a little slower. He had trouble getting his socks on because his feet were still wet. It must be a bummer for him to always be slower and smaller than his brothers. I thought about my experience with Coach Carpenter and my realization that it didn't matter what your body looked like.

Who cared if I hung out with a smaller kid?

"How old are you?" I asked.

"I'm eleven."

Last summer I was the age that he was now. He wasn't a baby at all. He just couldn't keep up with Grant and Austin, and it made him seem younger.

"What's your name?"

The kid looked at me suspiciously. "Brady."

"Brady Clairmont," I said. "That kinda sounds like Baby Clairmont."

He made a face. "I like being called Brady better."

Like how my dad called me Joe. I liked that better than Joey. "Okay." I smiled.

Brady stood up and wiped the grass off his bum. He gave me a weird look. "Bye," he said at last.

"Bye, Brady."

He smiled before running off.

Good deed done for the day. It made me feel a little better about swimming when I wasn't supposed to. I flung an arm over my face to keep the sun out of my eyes. I let my body sink deeper into the grass and enjoyed the warmth of the sun on my skin. I was lucky I only had one cracked rib. When I was finally dry, I headed home.

Nothing to do. No pressure of business for the

day. No golf or tennis lessons to attend.

I opened my front door.

Everything was quiet. Christine was at a friend's house.

Oh, life was perfect. Life was—

Life was interrupted by a flash of color twirling through the backyard. Mom was dancing outside. It was bad enough that she did the cha-cha around the kitchen, but now the neighbors could see her from their second-story windows.

I rushed to the sliding glass door, and my mouth dropped open.

She wasn't dancing alone.

Her partner was my new Turbo Drench 3000.

Mom sashayed beside her flowerbeds, squirting water into the dirt. Then she leaped over a large rock, shimmied next to a potted plant, and twirled before squirting the roots.

I flung the door open. "Mom."

"What?" She did a pirouette and lifted my gun—*my gun*—to water her hanging basket.

"Mom!"

"What?" She mambo'd over to her rosebush.

"*Mom!*"

Mom gave me a grin. Then, after a running

start, she pushed off the ground and sailed Superman-style above the earth. She seemed to float there longer than possible. She didn't reposition to land on her feet—she was going to break a rib, too—but at the last moment, she reached for the ground with her hands, tucked her chin to her chest, and rolled from a somersault up onto her feet facing me, gun pointing to the sky in a classic secret-agent pose. "Hi," she said.

I stood there. That was the coolest thing I'd ever seen my mother do. "What *was* that?"

"That was a dive roll. I could teach you how to do one."

"Oh, yeah."

"Or you could take gymnastics."

Oh, no. Not another class. I changed the subject. "Mom, why do you have my new gun?"

Mom looked at the weapon in her hand as if she were surprised to see it. "Oh, our water hose has a hole in it. This came in the mail today, and I figured it would work."

"No, no, no. I paid for it, Mom."

"And who paid for golf camp and tennis lessons?"

I groaned. "I never asked you to."

"Do you know why I signed you up for tennis? Because Chance's mom told me not to. She said you would create a ruckus."

My rib throbbed again. Chance's mom was right. I was full of hijinks that caused ruckuses.

Mom put her arm around me. "I just want you to find something that you are good at other than causing trouble."

I closed my eyes. I was good at having fun. Why did parents always confuse having fun with causing trouble?

Still holding my gun, Mom ushered me into the house. "That's why we should sign you up for gymnastics."

I sunk into a chair at the table. "I'm not good at sports. They're hard for me. I hate them."

Mom sat down across from me. "I think gymnastics would be different. You would get to jump and tumble and flip through the air. You know, kind of like those girls on the flying trapeze at the circus."

She did make it sound exciting. And what about my little flip off the rope swing? Maybe I would be good at gymnastics. "I don't know."

Mom held up the Turbo Drench. "I'll give you

81

your gun back."

I narrowed my eyes. That was so not fair. "Fine."

Mom's face lit up like it did when she was on stage in the spotlight. "Goody." She placed my gun on the table and slid it over to me.

I caressed it, running my hand along the plastic yellow barrel. Solemnly, I lifted it into my arms.

It was huge.

I hugged it to me. Parker hadn't messed up after all. "Where's my slingshot?"

Mom shook her head. "It didn't come today."

"But I ordered them together."

Mom shrugged. She was already online looking up the number for the gymnastics center. "You could see if the Lancasters have it."

Parker *did* mess up.

I imagined myself hurling water balloons at his windshield. Or I could squirt him with Kool-Aid and get him all sticky.

Hopefully it would get him to quit his job. He was a terrible mailman.

I tensed as I walked down the sidewalk to Isabelle's front door. I hated having to ask her for something. Maybe her mom would answer the door. Maybe not.

Isabelle swung the door open but didn't say anything. One skinny eyebrow lifted in a challenge.

"Hi." I cleared my throat. "Did you guys get a package in the mail for me today?"

Isabelle didn't move. "What's in it?"

I scowled. "None of your business."

"If you want to get it back, it is."

"It's a bunch of slugs."

"You don't scare me. I've licked a slug before."

That was gross, but I was jealous. Was I the only one in the world who hadn't licked a slug? "All right, it's a water balloon slingshot."

"Cool." Isabelle looked as if she was about to slam the door in my face so she could go play with my new toy.

"Can I have it?"

Isabelle cocked her head to one side. "What do I get in return?"

"You can get out of my way." Steam must have been coming out of my ears like cartoon characters when they got mad.

Dan, Dan, the Ice Cream Man's truck rolled past our houses, the familiar tune tinkling through the air.

"Buy me an ice cream cone."

"Look, I don't have any money." And I had to buy ice cream for Chance if I lost the bet …

That was it!

"I do have a secret I can tell you."

Isabelle's eyes got big. "Okay. What's your secret?"

"You'll give me my slingshot?"

"Yes. What's the secret?"

So I told her. Well, not everything. I certainly didn't tell her about the kiss.

Chapter Ten:

Weekend Warrior

"Supply and demand, my boy." Dad put down the newspaper and gave me his full attention.

"Huh?"

He rubbed his hands together. "You asked for an economics lesson."

What was economics? "No, I didn't. I just want to know how I can make more money water fighting."

"Exactly." Dad stood up.

I expected him to wipe off Mom's theater schedule from our chalkboard and start drawing pie charts.

Somehow he contained himself. "Say there are two cupcakes left for dessert tonight."

I was confused already. "Since when does Mom bake cupcakes?" She'd made me bran muffins for my last birthday.

"Okay, say Mom is gone. I have two cupcakes. You and Christine have to buy them from me. How much would you pay?" He placed his hands on the back of a chair and leaned forward.

"Umm ... a quarter?"

Christine had recently earned two quarters from Mom for videotaping Mom's dance practice in the living room.

"Okay." Dad pushed off and paced around the table. "But what if you each had a friend over for dinner and there were still only two cupcakes left?"

I sat up straighter. "Then I would buy them both for Chance and me."

Dad narrowed his eyes. "How much would you pay?"

I shrugged. "I guess I would have to pay more than Christine could. I'd pay fifty cents a cupcake." If I weren't still in debt.

Dad slapped his palm on the table. "So what does that teach you?"

I lifted my eyebrows. "Cupcakes can be expensive?"

Dad laughed and sat back down. "The more people that want a product—or a service, in your case—the more money they will pay for it."

I rested my elbow on the table, and my chin on my fist. "So where do I get all these people?"

Dad gave me a look that said I should be able

to figure it out. "When are there the most people at the park?"

I thought about Chance's baseball games. "Weekends. During sporting events."

"So?" Dad turned his body sideways to face mine. "How can you make more money water fighting?"

I looked out the window.

Cars fought over parking spaces in front of the playground.

"I should go to work. And I should raise my prices."

Dad nodded wisely. "You're going to be a hot commodity on a day like this."

Brilliant. Swinging my backpack over my shoulders, I grabbed my Turbo Drench 3000 and my slingshot. "See ya."

Dad gave me a thumbs up as I ran out the door.

Displaying my sign at the picnic table closest to the baseball diamond, I pulled a magic marker out of the front pouch and crossed out some of my prices. A cup of water stayed at fifty cents and a simple water balloon still only cost seventy-five cents, but I added the balloon slingshot at one dollar. The Turbo Drench was definitely worth a dollar and twenty-five cents. I had tossed the Mega Drench in my garbage can that morning. To get customers' attention, I juggled some balloons.

Two teenagers sat lazily on top of a picnic bench nearby. They didn't seem the least bit interested in my performance.

Behind them, two moms walked with a toddler between them. "I don't know how the boys are supposed to play baseball in this heat," the one with short hair said, propping sunglasses on the top of her head as she stepped into the shade.

Boise was high desert. No cacti or sand dunes, but also no rain during the scorching summers.

"I know," said the woman with long red hair. "They're not only burning up, they're dehydrated."

Dehydrated? Lacking in water? Maybe I could help.

The redhead paused at a drinking fountain and hoisted the toddler up to get a drink.

I strutted over. "Excuse me, ladies," I said in my most professional voice. "I overheard you talking and thought I might offer my assistance."

They both turned to look at me. Then they looked at each other.

Facing me again, the short-haired woman asked slowly, "What kind of assistance?"

I resumed my water balloon juggling. "My name is Joey Michaels. I'm a water fight professional, and for just a small price I could help your children and their team cool off from the heat."

"A water fight professional," mused the red-headed woman. "So you could do what? Throw water balloons at our boys?"

"I have cups of water, water balloons, and a water gun." I mentally crossed my fingers. If I got these moms to hire me, the whole team would become potential clients.

The women looked at each other again.

"Do you think the kids would like that?" asked one.

Their gazes shifted to the baseball diamond behind me.

The pitcher shielded his eyes, preparing for the pitch. The basemen stood planted to their spots with arms hanging heavily, and the outfielders moved around slowly as if through sludge.

"They need something to liven up the game." The other lady looked back at me. "I'm not sure

89

about the water balloons. Let's start with a cup of water for all the players."

Woohoo. "How many players?" I tried to keep the excitement out of my voice.

The woman slipped her purse off her shoulder. "Ten. How much will that cost?"

"Five dollars, ma'am." My feet itched to do a jig. My biggest sale yet. And how easy was it to fill up ten cups of water?

The woman handed me a five-dollar bill. "We're the Rangers. Let me warn the coach first. Next time we're up to bat, you can dump a cup of water on each of the players."

Yes! I nodded and hurried off to grab my paper cups. As I jogged back to the field, the Rangers struck out a batter for the third out. Time for business. A kid with bright orange hair caught my eye.

He plopped a helmet on top of his head and picked up an aluminum bat. Wiping sweat from his forehead, he rolled his shoulders back.

My first target. I couldn't call him a victim, because in a sense, I was helping his team. "Hey, buddy." I smiled at him. "Are you hot?"

"I'm dying."

"I can help." I angled the cup of water his direction and let gravity do the rest.

"Ah!" he shrieked. Then, as the breeze cooled his dripping skin, he repeated the sound, but in a refreshing way. "Ah … can you do that again?"

"Sorry, I've only been paid to dump each player with one cup."

"Well." He shrugged. "It was worth it."

After jogging into the batter's box, he practiced swinging with renewed vigor. So what if the dust stuck to him and turned to mud? He'd gotten a moment's relief from the searing sun.

Other Rangers had seen the kid get splashed.

"My turn," called a big kid. He reminded me of Chance—large for his age.

"Oh, me too," said a black kid.

They lined up for me to soak them. Work had never been so easy. And it was awesome watching them explode with energy. The first Ranger up to bat hit the ball out of the park.

"Way to go, Rangers," yelled parents in the crowd.

"Hey, kid," called the coach from the other team.

Was he talking to me?

"Yeah, you. Get over here."

I trotted behind the bleachers, hoping for more business.

The coach for the Angels didn't let me down. "I want you to douse my team."

"Well, sir," I said, trying to hide a grin. "I'm out of paper cups, but for a dollar twenty-five I can squirt one of your guys with my water gun."

"One dollar and twenty-five cents per player? That's preposterous."

My excitement faded. Dad's suggestion had let me down. I turned to go.

"Wait," a kid behind the coach called.

I stopped and looked over my shoulder. It was Chance.

"What Joey is offering is better than steroids."

My jaw dropped. Chance's words might help me win the bet.

He motioned me to join him in the dugout. "Come on, Coach. Just for the players up to bat. You saw how it helped the Rangers."

The Coach shrugged and dug into his pocket for some cash. "Anything for Zabransky."

"Hey," yelled the first mom—the one with sunglasses—from the bleachers. "We want the water fight professional back."

"He's mine now," hollered the coach.

Me, a double agent—playing both sides. But as Chance's best friend, I should be helping out his team.

The red-headed mom stood up and waved a ten-dollar bill overhead. "I'll pay to have a water balloon tossed at each of our players."

My mental cash register rang up to seven dollars and fifty cents. Not quite what Chance's coach was offering. "Sorry," I called back. "The Angels outbid you."

The woman jumped off the side of the bleachers and headed my way. "We're down by one. Pump that water gun, and start coolin' off the Rangers. I'll pay you whatever you want."

The world around me faded at her words, and I floated on a fluffy cloud in heaven—only the Angels were playing baseball instead of harps.

Ah, yes. Supply and demand. I was more like my dad than I realized. "Sorry, Chance."

Chapter Eleven:
Raising the Bar

Mom turned our car into the huge parking lot of the gymnastics center. "Tuck your T-shirt into your shorts."

Ugh. A dress code. "You're not going to watch, are you?" She hadn't stayed to watch golf or tennis, but that might have been because Chance was there. And that was before I got into trouble.

"No." Mom tapped her hand against the steering wheel to the music playing on the radio. Her head swayed side to side. "I've got to buy some groceries."

By groceries she meant tofu, bean sprouts, and asparagus. Yummy.

She pulled the car next to the main door for Tumble Time. "This is just a trial class. Dad told me not to spend any more money on classes unless you love them and commit to attending." She squeezed my hand as I started to climb out. "I know you'll love it."

"Sure, Mom."

"Bye, Twinkle Toes," Christine called from the backseat.

I stuck my tongue out at her. Babyish, I know, but what could I say? I was taking gymnastics. After trudging through the main lobby, I entered a huge warehouse-sized room.

Trampolines lined the front wall next to a pit filled with sponge rectangles. Rows of balance beams stuck out from the back wall beside a bunch of bars all adjusted to different heights. The front part of the gym was empty—just floor space.

My chest tightened in excitement.

"Joey Michaels?" A man motioned me over. He had dark hair and an accent. And huge arms.

I stared at his rock-hard shoulders. Wow. I doubted Christine would dare call him Twinkle Toes.

"That's me." I walked over to a group of boys sitting in a circle.

One kid had a mischievous glint in his eye.

I sat next to him.

"Straddle stretch," said my new coach.

The other boys spread their legs wide.

I pulled mine apart. Ow. I couldn't even keep my legs straight.

"Pike."

We swung our legs together and leaned forward. Again, ow.

"Tripod."

The boys rolled to their knees, placed their heads on the floor, lifted their knees, and then rested them on their elbows. Toes touched together above their rears.

I rolled to my knees and balanced on my head. I could do it.

"Headstand."

The boys lifted their legs straight to the ceiling.

I extended my legs. Awesome.

"Whoever holds it the longest, gets to jump on the trampoline first," said Coach.

My face grew hot as blood rushed to my head. How long could I stay up?

The kid next to me landed on the floor with a thud. He didn't seem to care that he was the first one to fall.

How cool was it that even though I was the new student, I had already beaten someone? That was probably how Chance felt whenever he played a new sport.

Swish. The other kid next to me rolled gracefully

into a somersault.

Two down, three to go. My stomach muscles heated up as I maintained my balance.

Crash. Boom. A third kid lost his balance and knocked over the gymnast next to him.

It was down to me and one other boy. The top of my head felt as if it were caving in, but I didn't give up.

"We're down to two," announced Coach.

I already knew that, but it was nice to be recognized.

One of my legs drooped toward the floor. All the pressure shifted into my right arm.

"One of you will get to jump on the trampoline first." Coach walked between us.

His reminder worked. I snapped my leg back up to the ceiling and regained my balance.

"Hey!" A shout, then a thud.

"Joey wins."

I clumsily dropped to my knees and closed my eyes until the stars and static faded.

"Not fair," said the kid that almost beat me. "Eric pushed me."

I glanced at Eric. He was the one I'd sat next to. I liked him even more now.

His eyes sparkled as Coach admonished him.

Did he ever get accused of causing a ruckus? It would be nice not to be the only one full of hijinks.

"Joey, you're up." Coach strutted over to the trampoline.

I had no idea what I was doing, but I couldn't wait to do it. I climbed on the trampoline and sprung into the air.

Coach taught me how to stop by bending my knees, sticking my bum out, and holding my hands in front of me.

My legs absorbed the bounce and I was able to stay in place.

"Good." Coach explained how to do a seat drop, back drop, and belly flop.

The belly flop was my favorite. I could land on my stomach, spring into the air with my arms and legs tucked in tightly, and twist around to land on my stomach facing the other direction. I could even go from a seat drop to a belly flop by straddling my legs and whipping them around from in front of me to behind me.

"Next," said Coach.

I didn't want to get off. I pointed to a harness-type thing suspended from the ceiling. "Can't I try that out?"

Coach didn't smile. Maybe he never smiled. "You must earn it."

Usually that would be a bad thing, but if "earning it" meant more belly flops and headstands, I was totally in. The other boys had their chance to jump, then we lined up behind the foam pit.

I pictured myself doing a cannonball, but all Coach wanted us to do was stand with our backs to the pit, cross our arms, and free fall.

The kid who almost beat me—should have beaten me—in the headstand competition, got to go first this time. He threw himself backward. At the last second, he looked over his shoulder and buckled.

Coach clicked his tongue.

"It's harder than it looks," the boy muttered to me as he climbed out.

Okay. I lined up with my back to the pit, crossed my arms, and dropped straight back. Simple. Awesome. Simply awesome.

I wanted to do it again, but Coach ordered us to do somersaults. I rolled on the floor just as easily as I rolled my eyes.

Coach lined us up at the end of the floor and demonstrated a run, a jump, and a roll.

I ran. I jumped. I rolled.

Coach lined us up again. He had a couple of kids repeat the series, but when it was my turn he held up his hand. This time he ran, dove, and rolled.

Yes. I did my very first dive roll. Oh yeah, I felt like Superman. All I needed was a red cape.

For the remainder of the class, Coach ran us through an obstacle course.

I negotiated the setup as if I was being timed.

Coach shook his head at me. "Slower. Stronger. Legs straight. Point your toes."

A little while later, Eric was showing me how to swing on the bar when a few girls began to trickle in. "They're here for the next class."

A couple girls practiced their splits and bridges. Then one stood and flipped over backward.

My mouth opened in awe. And envy. "I want to do that."

Eric looked over. "Back handsprings are hard. They take a lot of practice."

"Oh, yeah?" I didn't mind risking injury in the

attempt of a new trick. My blood pumped faster. I stepped away from the bars, took a deep breath, and threw myself backward. My hands touched the carpet, but my legs barely made it over. I landed in a frog squat. I stayed in the squat for a moment because my back felt as if it had been stretched through a taffy pull and my rib twinged.

"Wow." Eric grinned.

Coach wasn't impressed. "Joey," he yelled, voice stern. "You may only do what I tell you to."

He sounded like a dictator.

Maybe he was from Cuba and was used to all that.

"So?" a female voice said behind me. "You're getting into trouble already, Joey?"

I spun around.

Isabelle stood with one hand on a bar. She had on some sparkly black outfit that looked like a swimming suit with shorts attached.

I groaned. "What are *you* doing here?"

Isabelle tossed her ponytail. "I've been taking gymnastics since I was three."

Barf. "You come every week?"

Isabelle nodded.

My stomach grew nauseous. I couldn't very well

101

tumble with a sick stomach. That was it. If Isabelle came to gymnastics every week, then I was never coming back.

Chapter Twelve:
Starlight, Star Bright,
Stars Shine on the Stage Tonight

The Starlight Mountain Theatre was up in the mountains about an hour away from our home. That explained the "Mountain" part of its name. The "Starlight" part was a result of the owner not putting a roof on the building. With such a combination, it was important to bring lots of bug spray. Unfortunately, the bug spray didn't take care of the pest that was bugging me.

"I know Joey's secret," Isabelle sang in my ear as we took our seats in the front row.

"Zip it," I whispered.

Dad let Christine and me both invite friends to the opening night of Mom's performance. Chance had refused to come until he found out we were camping overnight and white-water rafting in the morning. The next day's adventure would make a little musical theater bearable.

Christine leaned in toward Isabelle. "What

secret?"

Isabelle's eyes sparkled.

I glared. "There's no secret," I snapped. No secret she needed to know.

Dad stared at me. "What secret?"

My heart skipped a beat. My mind raced. What could I say? I opened my mouth.

Out came music. Well, not really. It just sounded that way because the pre-show performance started.

Mom spun onto stage. She had on a long dress and the top part of her hair was swept back into a knot. Singing, she sashayed into the crowd, winking at Dad as she passed us to climb up the bleacher-like rows.

Her voice sounded flirty. Ick. It was some song from *Annie Get Your Gun*. She would star in that play later on in the summer.

"She looks beautiful," Isabelle murmured.

I rolled my eyes.

Chance slumped in his seat, completely bored.

I twisted around just in time to see Mom sit on some stranger's lap. "Dad," I choked.

Dad reached over Chance to squeeze my knee as if to say, *It's okay. She's making money.*

I gave him my bug eyes, and he chuckled.

Thankfully, Mom didn't cuddle up to any other men. She made her way back to stage and took a bow as everybody cheered.

Dad leaned over to me. "It's all an act, Joe. It's part of her job. She's going to kiss some young punk during the play, too."

I couldn't believe it. A kiss? Dad should be punching the "young punk's" lights out. But no, he was going to watch it happen with his children and their friends. How disturbing.

Chance chuckled at the look on my face. "Maybe you could take notes, Joey." He motioned with his head toward Isabelle, as if I needed a reminder that I had to kiss her if I lost the bet.

I spun to see if Isabelle had heard him.

No, she was giggling and pointing to the stage with Christine.

There was no way I was going to kiss that priss. I elbowed my best friend to keep him quiet. "Plays are dumb. You will never find me on stage pretending to be somebody's boyfriend." I turned back to the pre-show.

A guy and a girl faced each other, acting as if they used to date and had just run into each other

105

again.

"So?" asked the guy. "Do you have a boyfriend now?"

"Um … yeah," said the girl. "What about you? Are you dating anyone?"

"Uh … yes. And she's here tonight to watch me perform." He looked out into the audience. "There she is." He pointed past us. After jumping off the stage, he grabbed a lady from the audience and pulled her to her feet in front of everyone.

I laughed. Poor woman.

"This is my girlfriend." He presented her to the actress on stage.

"Well," the actress put her hands on her hips. "My boyfriend is here tonight, too. She walked toward our row of chairs looking at Dad.

I laughed even louder. It would be hilarious if he had to go on stage.

She grabbed Dad's shoulder. "This is my boyfriend. No." She let go of his arm and reached past him for Chance. "This is my … oh, wait …" She stepped into our row and put her hand on my arm. "This is my boyfriend."

Christine and Isabelle screamed with giggles.

I shot Dad a help-me look, but he was laughing

too.

Chance patted me on the back as I passed—just glad the girl had let go of him, I'm sure.

I trudged up the steps into the spotlight.

The girl proudly presented me to the boy on stage.

"So what's his name?" The boy crossed his arms and puffed up his chest.

"His name is …" she turned and stage-whispered to me, "What's your name?"

"Joe."

The girl put her arm around me. "His name is Joe—the perfect name for my new beau."

"Joe-beau," the guy called me.

Dad grinned from ear to ear.

Chance rocked in his seat with laughter.

I was never going to hear the end of this.

"What does Joe-beau do?"

I opened my mouth to respond, but my "girlfriend" answered for me. "He's a circus performer."

Not a bad answer.

"Is he a clown?" challenged the guy.

"No," the girl retorted. "He's … he's …" she turned to me. "Just show him what you do,

107

honey."

The crowd roared then clapped for me.

"Come on, Joey," yelled Christine and Isabelle, now my biggest fans.

Chance pumped the air with his fist. "Ooh, ooh, ooh," he grunted.

Dad pointed at me as if to say, *That's my boy*. He was probably wondering how soon until I could get an acting job and start making money for him.

My mom peeked at me from side stage.

I cracked my neck and strutted forward. I motioned for my "girlfriend" and the other couple to step back. Once I faced the length of the stage, I took a few running steps, leaped into the air, and fell into a perfect dive roll. I rose and raised my arms overhead in victory.

Dad jumped to his feet first.

The rest of our row followed. Then the entire theater stood up. A wolf whistle split the air.

Mom's jaw dropped.

My "girlfriend" kissed me on the cheek, and my face grew hot.

"So?" She turned back to the other guy. "Can your girlfriend beat that?"

I missed the rest of our act. I think the woman

was supposed to be a singer, but I didn't listen to her belt out any of the lyrics from "The Star-spangled Banner." I was too busy reliving my moment in my head. I missed the whole first half of the play, as well.

The sky was starting to get darker and we all huddled under blankets.

Mom appeared in front of us during the intermission. "Do you guys want popcorn?" Words I never expected to come out of her mouth.

"Who are you?" I asked.

Mom smiled. "The whole cast has to sell snacks." She held a carton filled with bags of popcorn. "Don't worry though. We're having fish for breakfast."

Chance sent me a worried look. My friends forgot how weird Mom was.

"If we catch any," I explained to him. "Otherwise we have cereal and fruit."

Dad doled out the money, and we each grabbed a bag of popcorn. Were we on some strange new planet? Mom offering us popcorn, Dad spending money that he didn't have to, me getting cheered for instead of Chance? I never wanted to leave.

109

Mom stopped the girl who had played my "girlfriend" on stage. "Olivia, this is my son," she said.

Olivia blew me a kiss. "He's a cutie."

Isabelle and Christine giggled.

I fake gagged.

Mom narrowed her eyes at my actions. "Yeah, real cute." Then her face brightened. "But he sure can tumble. You're good, Joey. Why don't you want to sign up for gymnastics?"

I glanced sideways at Isabelle to see if she was listening.

She was. "He can do a back handspring, too," she chimed in.

Mom shook her head as if she were trying to wake up from a dream. "You can do a back handspring? You only took one class."

"Yeah." I looked away.

The bad guy from the play made his way down our row. He was selling drinks with his popcorn.

"Can I have a drink, Mom?"

"Ask your dad. He's the one with the money." She moved off with Olivia to sell popcorn to some other kids.

Bad Guy stopped in front of me. He wore a

black wig and his jacket was just as dark. His beady eyes narrowed under thin eyebrows. "Where did you get your popcorn?" he asked in a menacing voice.

I couldn't help smiling. "My mom," I said.

"You're only supposed to buy popcorn from me," he growled.

I pointed at Dad. "He's the one with the money. We've already bought popcorn, but we need some drinks."

Bad Guy looked me up and down. "Very well," he said at last.

Dad bought drinks from him.

"I wish I could take him home," I whispered to Chance. "He just got Dad to spend even more money."

Up on stage, two college-aged kids wearing powdered wigs like George Washington's announced a two-for-one deal. "Buy one piece of licorice, get two kisses free."

Girls squealed.

Christine leaped out of her chair. "Please, Daddy, can I have some licorice?"

"Christine." I acted horrified. "It would break Parker's heart if you let those guys kiss you."

111

Christine swatted at me but missed because I sat back in shock.

Dad was pulling out his wallet again?

What?

He handed the girls two dollar bills.

Isabelle and Christine stood on their seats and waved the money in the air to get the actors' attention.

The teenagers came running over.

"Or maybe," Chance said quietly, "it will break your heart when the guys kiss Isabelle."

That time *I* swatted and missed.

Chapter Thirteen:
Man Overboard

I zipped my wetsuit up to my chin and clipped the life jacket together across my chest. I'd floated the Boise River before, but this was the big time. We even had a guide.

Wading into the water, we all wobbled for a moment as we tried to climb into the unstable raft. Chance and I straddled the right side with Mom behind us, and Dad sat with the girls across from us. Our guide, Mitch, gave us all paddles and demonstrated different techniques—kind of like Coach Carpenter's tennis lesson, except this time I listened.

"Oh, man, I wish I'd brought my water gun." I looked across the expanse before us.

"Joe," Dad scolded. "I think we are going to get wet enough without your help."

"Let me know if you don't." I slapped the river with my paddle and sprayed water across the raft.

The girls shrieked.

"There will be time for that later," Mitch said as

he took a seat in the rear of the raft. "We've got a rapid coming. You guys ready?"

"Woohoo," I hollered. I lifted my oar overhead like a barbell.

"Here we go." Mitch's voice trailed off as the raft slipped down a small slope with a splash. "Right side, row hard."

That was me. I brought my oar down and pushed against the waves. A cold shower of water blasted me in the face as the raft nearly bent in half.

"Go, go, go," shouted Mitch. "There's a cave on the other side just around this bend. Let's see if we can get to it."

Chance's muscles bunched in his shoulders. "Let's go, people."

"Argh," I grunted as if I were a pirate.

Isabelle laughed. "Ahoy, me mateys. Buried treasure ahead." She had a pretty good pirate voice going on.

Mom noticed, too. "Isabelle, you should be an actress." She stopped rowing.

"Mom," I yelled.

The current threatened to take us right past the dark spot in the wall of rock. Water roared and crashed.

Chance and I stuck our paddles in deep and tried to maneuver closer to the hiding place.

The nose of our raft made it into the opening, but the back half got bounced around as the river tried to pull us downstream.

Mitch yelled something I couldn't hear over the noise.

"What?"

Mitch pointed past me.

What was he pointing at? It was just a wall of rock.

I started to look back at Mitch again, but Isabelle dove toward me.

She stretched on her stomach across the front of the raft and grabbed onto the roots of a shrub growing overhead. "Help."

I reached up as well, and together we pulled the raft into the cave.

The quietness of the cavern muffled the sound of the river and it felt as if headphones covered my ears. The reflection from the sun shining on the water made rippling patterns on the damp cave walls. The strange light turned Isabelle's high ponytail into the glow of a halo.

115

I knew she wasn't an angel, but she wasn't a typical girl either because she could work. She climbed back to her spot on the other side of the raft.

I was impressed. But I didn't want to sound impressed. "Shiver me timbers," I said.

Mom laughed. "This is beautiful—better than buried treasure. Good work, Captain Lancaster and Captain Michaels."

Chance glanced over his shoulder at me. "Shiver me timbers?" he teased.

I turned away to ignore him and accidentally met Isabelle's gaze.

She smiled.

I smiled back. Maybe I could be friends with a girl.

Mom sang lyrics from "Yo Ho (A Pirate's Life for Me)." It echoed off the walls, sounding eerie.

"Are you ready for more?" Dad asked from his position behind Isabelle.

"Bring it on." The cave was pretty and peaceful. I could only handle that for so long.

"Then let's go." Mitch spun the raft around and shoved off a rock.

The rapids grabbed us and wouldn't let go. It

116

was a wild ride—probably as close to a bucking bronco as I would ever get.

I hung on with one hand and waved the paddle in the air with the other. "Yee-haw!" I'd gone from a pirate to a cowboy in a matter of seconds.

Mitch yelled directions and we tried to follow. Bumping into a rock that Mitch told us to avoid made us spin around and sent us backward down a water slide-like slope. Waves slapped us in the face.

Christine screamed.

"Right side." Mitch ordered Chance, Mom, and me to row again.

Though my side was doing all the work, we got the raft headed the correct direction. Chance and I were good. We had everything under control. I decided to be a guide when I grew up. I was a natural. I was—

I was thrown out of the raft. Sitting down one moment then—*pop*. I bobbed in the water.

"Joey," Mom yelled.

The water swirled and pushed me away from the raft. Wow, I floated fast. I flipped over to my stomach and began to swim. The trees on either side of me raced by. I felt like an Olympian.

"Joey," Mitch yelled. "Remember what I said about leaning back and putting your feet in front of you."

Oh, yeah. I sat as if I were in a chair so my legs could keep me from getting slammed into any rocks. The water was freezing, but I was too excited to care.

"Hang on," Dad yelled. "The rough part is almost over."

Bummer. It should all be rough. It was white water, wasn't it?

The current slowed, loosening its grip on my

118

arms and legs. The waves stopped swooping over my head.

Dad and Mitch expertly rowed toward me. Mitch reached down, grabbed the back of my life jacket, and scooped me out of the water.

I flopped on the floor of the raft like a fish.

Mom helped me back into my spot. "You okay?"

I nodded.

"We call that fanny floating," Mitch told us.

Chance laughed. "I should have known Joey would be the first to fanny float."

I pushed on Chance's vest as if I was going to knock him in the water. "Watch it, or you'll be next."

We all drifted quietly for a few minutes. No waves. No rapids. Not even a tiny splash to entertain us.

I could fix that. Angling my oar toward the river I sliced off the top layer of water and sent it across the raft.

"Stop it, Joey. I don't want to get wet." Christine sent me a death glare.

Mitch chuckled from behind us. "I wouldn't start a water fight with the girls, Joey. You might lose."

I looked over my shoulder. "It's okay. I'm a water fight professional."

"Joey." This time Isabelle's voice called my name.

I turned to face my new friend, but she didn't even give me a chance to ask what she wanted. She just tried to drown me with a wall of water. I sputtered and wiped at my eyes.

Christine giggled with glee. "Some water fight professional you are."

Isabelle sat grinning at me with a bucket in her hands. "I figured you wouldn't mind since you're already wet."

She figured wrong. "Where did you get a bucket?" I demanded.

"Mitch."

My mouth hung open, and I stared at the guide. He'd just become the enemy.

Mitch laughed. "The bucket is usually used to bail out water."

They had ganged up on me? "Well, now I'm bailing out." I lifted my left leg over the side to join my right leg and slipped into the water. I fanny floated the rest of the way down the river.

Chapter Fourteen:
Top Secret

I stuck the stamp to the corner of the envelope. Inside was the apology I wrote to Coach Carpenter and a check from Dad for fifty dollars. I wished that were the end of it, but no, I still owed Dad twenty-two dollars more for the repair. There went a couple of good days of water fighting.

"Joey," Mom called from the kitchen. "Parker is coming. Get that letter out to the mailbox now. Tomorrow is the Fourth of July so there won't be any mail."

I'm sure Mom expected me to start running, but her words caused me to freeze. The next day was the Fourth of July? That meant it was my last chance to win the bet. I looked up toward the ceiling, trying to figure out how much I had to make to average over ten dollars an hour.

Mom stuck her head around the corner. "Now, Joey."

I shook away my thoughts and rushed outside. It was a waste of energy, though.

Parker sat idly parked by our curb.

I moseyed the rest of the way to our mailbox.

The bottom half of Parker's body was all that could be seen. He leaned into the back of the jeep and tossed envelopes about. It kind of reminded me of that crazy chef on "The Muppets."

"I've got something for you," I said.

Parker jerked and hit the back of his head on the steering wheel. "Hang on, little dude," he said before diving back into his mess.

I just stood there looking around. Where was Christine? She rarely missed a chance to make goo-goo eyes at Parker.

"So how did golf camp go?" Parker's voice echoed back to me.

"Uh … I got to drive a golf cart."

"Groovy." Parker sat on his heels and took my letter. "See, I told you it wouldn't be so bad."

"Actually …" I leaned against the mailbox. "I'm thinking about taking gymnastics."

Parker nodded, reminding me of a bobble head. "That's a tough sport."

I wrinkled my eyebrows together. I'd never thought of gymnastics as a sport before. Hey, that meant I was good at a sport. "There's just one problem though. This girl that I hate takes gymnastics, too."

Parker narrowed his eyes. "Do you really hate her? Or do you hate the fact that you like her?"

I sighed. "She's different than other girls. I started to think that maybe we could be friends, but then she dumped a bucket of water on my head."

Parker didn't laugh at me like I thought he would. "Whoa, dude. It sounds as if she's a girl you should have on your side."

I considered his idea. "Maybe. She might be fun. But I don't want her to be my girlfriend."

Parker shifted back into his seat to share his wisdom with me. "I hear ya. Girlfriends are a lot of work."

I wondered if Parker had a girlfriend. That was information Christine would pay me for. "Do you have one?"

"No way." Parker grinned.

I grinned back. "My little sister, Christine, thinks you're cute."

Parker opened his mouth to say something, but all the entire neighborhood heard at that moment was a scream from behind me.

123

I turned in time to see Christine's horrified face.

"Jo-ey!" she yelled, threw an ice cream cone at me, and ran toward the house, slamming the door behind her.

The ice cream stuck to my shirt. The cone fell to the ground.

I looked down at the blob then back up at Parker. "Oops. I guess I shouldn't have told you that."

Parker shrugged. "No worries."

I wanted to follow Parker's lead and shrug off my mistake. I mean, Christine threw her ice cream cone at me. How funny was that? But for some reason my stomach turned over like Mom in a dive roll.

"See ya, dude." With a wave, Parker sped away.

I jogged back to the house.

Mom stood in the entryway with arms folded across her chest. She frowned at me before turning toward the empty stairway. Then, doing a double take, her gaze swiveled back to my T-shirt. "Where did you get *ice cream*?" The way she said it, you'd think she caught me hijacking another golf cart. She disappeared into the kitchen and returned with

124

a paper towel to clean me up.

"Um …" I looked down. "It's Christine's. She threw it at me when I told Parker she thinks he's cute."

"Oh, Joey." Mom sighed. "So that's why she stormed up the stairs. Go up and apologize to her. I'll talk to her about the ice cream later."

I shivered at Mom's plan. Yes, I needed to apologize. It was the other part that worried me. I could imagine her buying a lie detector just to quiz us about our snacks. Goodbye, ice cream man. There went my will to work. As I climbed the stairs, my thoughts refocused on my job. The Fourth of July was huge for picnics. If I worked two hours and averaged twelve dollars an hour, I would win the bet. If not—

"You jerk." A bottle of nail polish ricocheted off the wall by my head. "I can't believe you told Parker I like him. I can never go outside again."

And I thought my mom was the dramatic one. I ducked as a stuffed cat sailed through the air. I dropped to the floor and did an army crawl into Christine's bedroom to avoid the pink hailstorm accosting me.

Christine jumped on top of her bed and

125

whacked me with a heart-shaped pillow.

"Stop it." I grabbed the pillow and ripped it out of her hands. "I'm sorry I told your secret, all right?"

"No. It's not all right. My secret was …" She mellowed down. "My secret." She spoke quietly and climbed off the bed. It scared me even more than Cannonball Christine.

"What?" I asked suspiciously.

Christine stood and headed for the door. "You told my secret, so I'm telling yours." She ran.

I dove after her and tackled her in the hallway. "Isabelle told you my secret?" That blabbermouth.

"Yeah." Christine kicked at me and clawed toward the stairs. "And I'm going to tell Mom."

"Don't you dare." I clung to her ankle. "Mom already knows you were eating ice cream today. If she finds out about the bet and that we buy ice cream all the time, she'll lock us in our bedrooms for the rest of the summer."

Christine paused. "You told her I bought ice cream?"

"I didn't have to. It was all over my shirt when I came in the house, thank you very much." I pulled Christine away from the stairway.

"That's your fault, too." She twisted around to poke me in the chest. "You owe me an ice cream cone."

Ridiculous.

She couldn't blame me.

I didn't make her toss her treat. I would never buy her another cone, but I might ... "Look, tomorrow is the last day of the bet. If I beat Chance, I'll share the out-of-this-world triple dip with you. As long as you don't tell Mom and Dad."

Christine narrowed her eyes. "You think you'll win?"

I nodded as much to convince myself as her. "I only have to make twenty-four dollars in two hours. With the park as crowded as it's going to be, that should be a snap. Maybe you could help me."

Christine pulled away and sat with legs crossed. "Maybe." She gave me an evil smile.

I didn't trust her. "You're not going to rat me out?"

"Don't worry about that." She stood up. "I've got other plans."

That didn't make me feel any better. "So we've

127

got a deal?"

Christine skipped back to her room. "I'll be ready to water fight in the morning."

Chapter Fifteen:
Fun with a Water Gun

I sat on the front step, pinching firecracker poppers from their sawdust packing and tossing them at anybody who walked by. I should have been hard at work at the park, but I was enjoying my lazy day. Mom actually let me sleep in then eat cereal at lunch time. And besides, my business would do better when the picnics were in full swing. That wouldn't happen for another couple of hours.

Or maybe I was putting off my job because I was scared.

I didn't want to lose the bet. I *couldn't* lose the bet. Just thinking about the possibility made the Grape-Nuts in my stomach feel as heavy as Dad's dumbbells. My favorite hobby was now about as fun as P.E. when Chance got to pick his team and he didn't pick me.

I looked up from my shoes in time to see Isabelle skip by. I threw a popper at her.

It landed on the sidewalk and didn't even pop.

Isabelle stomped on it. *Crack*. She walked over and sat next to me.

I scooted a couple of inches away.

She held out her hand as if I were going to give her some of my poppers.

"Get your own," I muttered without even looking at her.

"You're no fun."

What? I was the definition of fun. I opened my mouth to argue, but she pointed past me.

"Look."

I didn't see anything unusual—just a mail jeep zipping down a side street. "Did Parker knock over another mailbox?"

Isabelle stared at me as if I were an idiot. "It's the Fourth of July. Mailmen aren't supposed to work on holidays."

I laughed. "Have you met Parker?"

"Hey, guys," Christine walked around from the side of the house, pulling a wagon. She wore a headband with two boingy blue stars on top for the holiday. Her face looked patriotic as well, as if she'd just eaten one of those red, white, and blue Popsicles. In her wagon were a bunch of leftover birthday party supplies.

Isabelle smiled. "Are you having a tea party?"

"No ..." Christine bent down to pick up a bag of pink paper cups with princesses printed on them and a bag of pink balloons. "I'm a professional water fighter today."

I groaned. "No, Christine. I am not using pink cups and balloons for my business."

Christine bent down again to pick up a thick piece of cardboard with letters on it. "You're not. I am." Her sign read "Super Water Fight Professional."

I laughed. "Nobody is going to hire you. You throw like a girl."

"Maybe." Christine's lips curled up. "But I'm offering free lemonade to every customer."

I shook my head. "Whatever. You won't sell more than I will."

Christine's wagon squeaked as she started toward the park again. "I don't have to sell more than you. I just have to keep you from winning the bet."

I jumped to my feet. "What?" That was so not the deal. "Then I won't win any ice cream to share with you."

"Chance is going to share with me," she called

back. She looked both ways and crossed the street.

I couldn't believe it. My best friend and my very own sister were ganging up against me. "Go … go … lick a slug."

Christine smiled over her shoulder. "I licked a slug on a field trip in kindergarten. You're the only one who's never licked a slug."

"Ah!" I screamed like a girl. Obviously, I wasn't a girl, but I sure was a sissy. Everybody, including my little sister, had licked a slug. Everybody except me. I wanted to pull my hair out. My hands flew to the top of my head and, because I was still holding the open box of poppers, they all spilled out behind me and crackled on the cement.

Isabelle wiped the extra sawdust off my shoulder.

I whirled on her. "This is your fault. You told Christine my secret. I should have known I couldn't trust a girl." I stomped onto the front step and grabbed the doorknob. What was I going to do?

Isabelle stood up as well. She didn't sound angry when she spoke to me, just snobby. "Maybe if you treated girls nicer, we wouldn't hate you so much."

Her words were a slap in the face. Christine hated me. Isabelle hated me. It shouldn't bother me so much. They were girls after all. But lately all the boys I knew had been too busy playing sports to hang out.

I stormed upstairs to my room and grabbed my green grenade water balloons and everything that went with them. The pink princess water fighter would be no match for me.

💧 💧 💧

Christine poured lemonade at a picnic table across from where I usually set up business.

Well, she wasn't going to scare me away.

But all the families nearby hired her for their water fighting needs. Well, actually they hired her for entertainment because she couldn't hit a single target.

The roar of applause at her latest attempt burned in my ears. Grabbing my backpack, I started stuffing everything in. I would have to set up elsewhere if I were to win the bet. My frustration boiled over like a pot of Mom's nasty soup.

Chance plopped down on the bench at my

133

table. "How's it going?" He grinned.

The cheater. "How do you think it's going?"

Chance spread his arms behind him along the table. "I think your baby sister stole your business."

"Way to send her to do your dirty work." I slung my pack over a shoulder.

Chance eyed my movements. "So you're going to set up somewhere else?"

I grunted in reply and turned away.

"Hmm …" Chance's musings stopped me in my tracks. "Christine told me that you needed to make twenty-four dollars in two hours."

I glanced back over my shoulder. "Yeah."

"And you've already been here one hour, right?"

My hope sank as if it had just gone off the Double Trouble slide at Roaring Springs.

"Have fun." Chance stood and jogged away as if he didn't have a care in the world.

I slumped down in the spot Chance had vacated and stared numbly at the table belonging to the "Super Water Fight Professional." The words on her sign blurred together. I blinked to clear my head and focus.

Her prices were lower than mine. I hadn't even noticed that earlier. Cup of water: twenty-five cents. Water Balloon: fifty cents. Water gun: seventy-five cents.

Water gun? Where did she get a water gun? My head jerked toward a peal of laughter.

A giggling teenage girl dripped with water.

Next to her stood Christine holding my old Mega Drench pointed directly at a high school boy. She must not have known that the gun shot off to the right, but she shouldn't have even had my gun in the first place.

"Christine," I yelled as she lugged the huge water gun back toward her table. "You stole my water gun."

"It was in the garbage," she said easily.

What made me the maddest was that she was right. It was as if I'd sabotaged myself. I told Isabelle my secret, I made Christine upset by telling *her* secret, and I'd put the water gun in the garbage can because I didn't want it anymore. What a mess. But since I was the one who made the mess, I had to be the one to clean it up. First off, I would get rid of my sister.

Unzipping my backpack, I pulled out a water

135

balloon and leaped onto the table. "Go home or get bombed," I yelled.

Christine looked up. Anybody watching would think she was completely innocent by the face she gave me.

I knew better. I snatched a second balloon.

Christine aimed her gun at me.

We fired at the same time.

As if in slow motion, the balloons inched their way toward her. Christine dove toward the ground when the water she shot from my old water gun did nothing more than water the flowers by my side. She wasn't fast enough.

Splat. Splat.

Her braids stuck to her face.

Ha.

She rolled to her table and grabbed some balloons, but her arm was no match for my slingshot.

I didn't even get wet.

Christine jumped up, and I couldn't tell if there were tears in her eyes or if all the water dripping down her face was from my attack. "I'm telling Mom," she shouted.

"What are you going to tell her?" I yelled at her

back as she ran away. "That we both threw water balloons at each other, only you have terrible aim?"

She disappeared behind some trees.

My conscience gnawed at my resolve. But at least she was gone so there would be no more competition. I could win the bet and make it up to my sister with some ice cream.

Except that next to Christine's picnic table stood Isabelle with arms crossed.

"What are you doing?" I asked suspiciously.

"I'm taking over for Christine. That was terrible what you just did to her."

I was terrible? No, I was the one who kept getting sucker punched. Chance, Christine, and now Isabelle.

"She's your little sister, Joey. You're supposed to protect her."

"No, somebody needs to protect me from her. She's in cahoots with Chance. They ganged up on me to keep me from winning the bet." I pictured Chance and Christine in the future with black trench coats and dark glasses. They were perfect candidates for organized crime. I was just the harmless victim.

137

Isabelle got busy refilling my old water gun. She smiled at the first person to walk by—an old lady with a bag of birdseed. "Are you interested in hiring a professional water fighter?"

The woman didn't hear very well. Isabelle had to repeat her question three times before the woman shook her fragile head and patted Isabelle's hand.

I watched in fascination, though I should have been moving my business like I planned to earlier. "That was silly," I called as the woman wobbled away. "You have to offer your services to people who might actually hire you."

Isabelle took a sip of Christine's lemonade. "Any more advice?"

She mocked me, but I thought back to all I had learned that summer anyway. "You could offer your service for free to get things going. When you have a high demand you can raise your prices. And you can offer discounts."

Isabelle lifted an eyebrow. "Discounts like the buy-one-get-two-free deal at The Starlight Mountain Theatre?"

My stomach cramped at the thought of the two licorice salesmen and their kisses. If I didn't win the bet, I was going to have to kiss Isabelle. And it would be all her fault. If she only knew … "Isabelle. Come here."

My prissy neighbor looked down her nose at me then started across the grass slowly. She kept my old water gun with her. "What?" she demanded when she reached my side.

I puffed out my cheeks like a blowfish, then let the air out all at once like a popped balloon.

"What?" she repeated.

"I didn't tell you everything about the bet." I studied curious brown eyes and freckles sprinkled over a nose where nostrils flared. "I told you that the winner gets the out-of-this-world triple dip. But I didn't tell you what the loser has to do."

"Tell me." Isabelle's eyes narrowed.

How do you explain to a girl that she is part of a bet? "The loser has to kiss you."

"Ack." Isabelle covered her mouth as if she had to throw up. "So either you or Chance has to kiss me?" she whispered when she regained control of her gag reflex.

I shrugged. I wished I could say it had been Chance's idea.

"This is horrible."

139

I looked down at my feet. "Sorry."

Isabelle grabbed my arm. "You have to win. I'll help you."

I'm sure my face lit up like the neon sign at the arcade. "Great. I've got an idea."

Putting my plan into action, she sneaked up on a couple of older kids, tossed cups of water at them, and took off running.

The kids yelled as she ran off.

That's when I stepped in to offer my services.

Every single time she did this, the people Isabelle soaked hired me to soak her in return. It was a dream job. I wished I'd thought of this gimmick at the beginning of the summer. Laughing, we met back up at the picnic table.

Isabelle looked as if she'd been jumping off the rope swing into the river. It was great. How often do you find a girl that would rather have you shoot her with the Turbo Drench 3000 than give her a little kiss? Parker was right. She was the kind of girl I should want on my side.

"So." Isabelle sprawled in the sun for a moment. "You've shot me with your water gun ten times, and used your slingshot seven times, right?"

"Yeah. And one cup of water." I counted my

money. "We've made over nineteen dollars. What time is it?"

Isabelle rolled over to her stomach and checked her watch. "Oh no, we only have five minutes to make five dollars. I don't think we can do it."

I jumped up. "We have to." I looked around frantically. "We just need to find a group of kids."

Isabelle groaned. "I don't know if I can run away from you anymore. I'm wiped out."

I grabbed Isabelle's hand and pulled her to her feet. "You can do it," I said. I handed her my Turbo Drench.

Isabelle's eyes got wide. "You'd let me use *your* water gun?"

I pointed toward the tree next to where the Clairmont family tossed horseshoes. "If you climb that tree and soak Grant, Austin, and Brady, their dad will pay me big bucks to get you back."

"Brady?" Isabelle paused. Apparently, she hadn't known Baby Clairmont's name either. Then, as if getting back to the game plan, she ran her hands over the gun the way I did when it first came in the mail. She pumped air into the pressure chamber. "All right. I'll give it all I've got."

I sat down.

141

Isabelle tucked the gun into the back of her pants. She jumped and grabbed a tree branch. Swinging back and forth, Isabelle kicked both legs forward and flipped them up and over the branch.

My mouth hung open.

With both arms straight, she held herself in the tree. Bending one knee, she lifted a foot on top of the branch next to her hands. Then she leaped like a frog to grab another branch higher overhead. This time she pulled her knees to her chest, flipped upside down, and hung by her legs. Reaching behind her back she pulled out the water gun and aimed at the family below.

142

Grant, Austin, and Brady shouted and hollered as they got doused with water, but I couldn't take my eyes off Isabelle. She finished her job, grabbed the branch with her hands, and flipped to the lower branch. The setting sun shined on her like a spotlight.

All of a sudden I imagined her flying through the air as if on a trapeze. She wasn't Prissy Izzy anymore. She was Isabelle the Amazing. I stood up as if to give an ovation.

Isabelle dropped to the ground and ran toward me.

What should I say? What should I do? Her words from earlier floated through my mind. She said she hated me because I wasn't nice. For the first time in my life, I wanted to be nice to a girl.

"Uh, hi …" I started stupidly, but Isabelle ran right past me.

"Go, Joe," she yelled.

Oh, yeah, my job. I jerked my head in the direction of the Clairmonts, and the brain fog faded.

Mr. Clairmont strode toward me. "Is she with you?" he asked, all business.

His boys bounced behind him.

143

Angela Ruth Strong

"Pay Joey to get her back, Dad." Grant wrung out his shirt.

"Was that Isabelle?" asked Austin.

I nodded.

"Use the slingshot," Brady chimed in.

Mr. Clairmont handed me a five dollar bill.

I stared at it. I'd done it. I'd won the bet with Chance. I wouldn't have to kiss Isabelle after all. But I did have to throw some water balloons at her. The funny thing was, she wanted me to.

Chapter Sixteen:
Signed, Sealed, Delivered

"So Chance has to kiss me, huh?"

I didn't say anything.

Isabelle tried to slide down the slide, but her wet clothing clung to the plastic. *Screech, screech.* She scooted forward a couple of times, then stood up. Squeezing drops of water out of her ponytail, she found a scrap of rubbery balloon in her hair.

That tended to happen when I cornered someone in the playground and completely drenched him or her.

"That was awesome. Maybe we should become business partners."

All I could do was smile.

"Come on. Let's go find Chance."

I followed behind her. I should have been elated about winning the bet, but instead my stomach tightened as if I were a water gun and somebody had pumped air pressure into *me*.

Isabelle shivered. "I should probably dry off before Chance buys us the out-of-this-world triple dip. I'm freezing."

"It's hot out here." I blabbed the first thing that came to my head. "You'll dry off fast." I looked down, feeling too weird to make eye contact.

Isabelle giggled and pranced through the grass. "There he is."

Chance crossed the street from the park toward our block.

Isabelle darted through the growing number of bodies crowding the park.

I jogged to keep up, leaping over a blanket with a toddler on it. Either she was really excited about ice cream or she wanted Chance to kiss her.

"He's never going to believe you beat him, Joe," Isabelle called back to me.

I don't know which part of Isabelle's statement made me more nervous—her elation that I beat Chance or the fact that she called me Joe. Joe. As if we were best friends or something.

"Chance, wait," she yelled.

Chance glanced over his shoulder and grinned once he saw me. He stuck his thumbs through his belt loops and waited for us on the corner between my house and his.

When we caught up with him, I bent over with

my hands on my knees and gulped air.

"Hi, Isabelle. Hey, Joey, you ready to pay up? I see Dan, Dan, the Ice Cream Man's truck parked over by the picnic shelters."

"Um ..." I sucked in another breath.

Isabelle took over. "Joey didn't lose, Chance. You did."

Chance gave an unsure half smile. "You've got to be kidding."

I opened my mouth but didn't get a word out.

Isabelle put her hand on my shoulder.

Goosebumps popped up on my arm as if I were the one soaking wet.

"It's true. I helped him, and he made twenty-four dollars in one hour. That's more than you've ever made mowing lawns."

Chance stood there speechless. Finally.

My turn to talk. I rubbed my shaky arms, feeling the way I had the first time I ever stood on top of the high dive at the swimming pool. And just like that time, I dove in. "I didn't win, Isabelle," I said.

Both heads spun and looked at me.

Isabelle blinked. "But you shot five water balloons at me. That costs five dollars exactly. And that's all you needed to win."

I grinned sheepishly. "I didn't take the money from Mr. Clairmont." Those five water balloons had been the highlight of my summer. There was no way I could charge a customer for that.

"What?" she squeaked.

"What?" Chance squeaked too. "That means you have to kiss Isabelle." His eyes widened. "You lost on purpose. You like Isabelle."

"Joe." Isabelle choked on the word in disbelief.

I stepped forward so that Isabelle and I were toe to toe. My heartbeat thumped in my ears.

Isabelle just stared at me.

I took a deep breath that could be felt through my entire body, then I smooshed my lips together, ready for my first kiss.

Isabelle ran. She shot off down the sidewalk.

Chance and I stared after her retreating back.

"Joey," Christine called to me with her sing-song you're-in-trouble voice. She glided up to us on her scooter, but I didn't even look at her.

I was too busy watching Isabelle run away. She was fast. I would never catch her.

"Mommy wants to talk to you."

I looked down at my sweet, weirditating little

sister. She'd actually helped me become friends with Isabelle. But I didn't have the time to talk at the moment, so she just needed to take her scooter and—

Take her scooter.

"Christine, I need your scooter." I grabbed her pink handlebars and stepped on the smiling face of a Barbie decal.

Before she could argue, I'd already rolled away.

I pushed off the pavement and the wind lifted my hair. Bumping over cracks in the sidewalk, I zoomed like a plane preparing for takeoff.

But Isabelle had gotten quite a head start and was still too far away.

Parker's mail jeep glided next to me. "Nice wheels, dude," he called.

I glanced sideways, and the sight of the mail jeep gave me an idea. "Parker, I need you to cut off Isabelle." I pointed.

Parker peered down the sidewalk. "You want me to stop that girl running away from you and your cute little scooter?"

I grinned. "Yes."

Parker shrugged. "Okay." He zipped away.

I pushed harder and watched as the mailman

passed Isabelle and turned into a driveway.

Isabelle slowed down since her escape route had been blocked. She stopped to catch her breath.

That was all the time I needed. As she looked back to see how far she'd gotten, I rolled beside her and bumped into the jeep. Dropping the scooter, I leaped in front of her so she couldn't circle around the vehicle and keep running.

"Joe, you're crazy." She panted.

"So are you," I blurted. "That's why I want to be your friend. You're not the prissy princess I thought you were." Then, before she could talk some sense into me, I leaned over and kissed her on the cheek.

Fireworks exploded overhead—not because it was an amazing kiss, but because it was Independence Day. Though the kiss wasn't as awkward as I thought it would be.

"Sweet." Parker leaned through the jeep's doorway, watching the whole scene.

I smiled like a goofball over at Parker. He was crazy, too, thank goodness. "You know you don't have to deliver mail today, don't you?" I asked.

"Huh?" Parker frowned at me. "So that's why I

was the first one at work."

Isabelle laughed, and it sounded good.

I joined her.

She smiled at me.

"Josiah Michaels."

Oh no. Mom was on the warpath.

"Your name is Josiah?" Isabelle lifted an eyebrow.

Most people didn't know my real name. "Josiah is a king in the Bible." I hoped that made me sound cooler.

Isabelle jabbed her chest with a thumb. "My middle name is Esther."

A queen? Better than a princess. "I think you're a lot of fun, but I don't want to be boyfriend/girlfriend."

Isabelle crossed her arms. "Good. Boyfriends are a lot of work."

Mom marched down the sidewalk. "I can't believe you attacked your little sister. You are grounded from the park for the rest of the summer, young man."

I guess I deserved that. "I'm sorry, Mom."

Chance joined us. "Maybe you can mow lawns now."

Never. That was ridiculous. I'd just purchased my water gun. My mind wandered back to the day the Turbo Drench came in the mail and Mom used it for watering her plants. I put my hands on my hips. "I won't mow lawns. No, I'm now Joey Michaels—Flower Watering Specialist."

Isabelle mimicked my posture. "Me too. Joe and I are good business partners."

Normally I would have argued. What boy wants a girl for a business partner? But now I knew that I was lucky to have Isabelle on my side.

Christine stomped past me and picked up her scooter. Glancing up at Parker, she purred like a kitten. Then turning to face us, she roared like a lion. "Mom," she said through clenched teeth. "You can't let him start a new business. He's a troublemaker."

I thought about all the trouble I had made. Crashing golf carts, wrecking wheelchairs, swiping scooters. I held my breath, waiting for Mom's judgment.

Mom looked me over. "I think a business would help him stay out of trouble. And he's good at it."

It was nice to feel as if I was good at something

for a change. Even if others thought it was goofy.

"No." Christine sassed. "That's just gazpacho." As soon as the word came out, her eyes grew wide and her hands flew up to cover her mouth.

Mom's forehead wrinkled. "Gazpacho?"

"I'm sorry." Christine whimpered. "I know I'm not supposed to say bad words."

"Gazpacho isn't a bad word. It's the name of that soup I made for you guys. Remember? You loved it. You ate it all."

Actually, Dad had dumped it down the sink. I better tell him to inform Mom of how we really felt about her soup before she made it again.

"Oh." Christine looked down in embarrassment. She didn't even turn around when Parker revved his engine.

"I'm out of here," our crazy mailman announced. "Have an awesome Independence Day."

Isabelle and I waved. I did feel pretty awesome. Christine, on the other hand, was still getting a lecture from Mom.

"Why would you want to say a bad word? It's offensive to others. And it's sad. Words that didn't used to be dirty are now used like curse words. It's very childish behavior, Christine, and I will not allow my children to talk that way."

"Joey, wasn't that your word?" whispered Chance.

Oops. "I guess I won't be saying it anymore." Linking arms with Chance and Isabelle, I took a step off the sidewalk.

"You're not supposed to go in the park," Isabelle reminded me as we crossed the street.

"I'm not." I headed down the sidewalk. "We'll just walk around the park to the ice cream man."

"Yes." Chance pulled his free elbow to his side in celebration. Now that the confusion was over, he could celebrate his victory.

"I've got nineteen dollars in my pocket." I mentally calculated my earnings the way Dad had taught me. "Two are for tithe, and two are for savings. But I'll use the rest to buy us all out-of-this-world triple dips."

Isabelle smiled at me. I smiled back at my new business partner. Maybe I'd lost the bet, but I'd won a friend.

The End

Dear Reader,

I was inspired to write this story when my son, Jordan, was in preschool. During a water fight at a church picnic, I could tell Jordan wanted to get involved but didn't know how. I gave him a cup of water and told him to dump it on somebody. Then someone else offered him a dollar to dump that same cup on me. I got wet, Jordan got paid, and he fell asleep that night holding onto his dollar bill. I said, "He's going to become a water fight professional," and thus, my story was born.

First, *The Water Fight Professional* came out in a book of short stories. Second, it got picked up to be used in English tests for students. Third, I'd written it into this novel and a publisher offered to buy it from me, but the publisher ended up going out of business. Now, as the book has finally made it into your hands, my Jordan is a high school student. And I just want you to know something: it was worth the wait.

So whether you write stories like I do, or if you play sports like Chance does, or if you have ideas for your own business like Joey does, keep at it. Keep doing what you love. Keep being the unique person you are. And though you will probably get discouraged or distracted somewhere along the way, if you don't give up, you too can create something so great that it's worth the wait.

I'd love to hear more about you and your dreams and what you learned from Joey. So come visit me at www.angelaruthstrong.com. I've also got some contests you can enter, games you can play, a book trailer you can watch, a series you won't want to miss, and an opportunity for you to join me in breaking the world record for biggest water balloon fight ever!

Keep fighting the good fight,
Angela Ruth Strong

Meet the Author

Angela Ruth Strong didn't run businesses as a kid, but in 7th grade she did start her own neighborhood newspaper. This childhood interest led to studying journalism at the University of Oregon and having one of her stories reach over half a million readers. To help other aspiring authors, Angela founded IDAhope Writers in Boise, Idaho, where she currently lives with her husband and three children (who always love a good water fight).

Acknowledgments

My kids, Jordan, Caitlin, and Lauren, for making my backyard a dangerous place to go if I don't want to get soaked. Besides inspiration for really fun stories, they bring me great joy.

My hubby, Jim Strong, for drawing the cutest slugs ever. And for making my life even more exciting than the books I write.

My parents, Mike and Ginger McGrath, who always encouraged me while teaching me accountability the way Joey's parents do in *The Water Fight Professional*. Well, not exactly the way Joey's parents do, though Mom did used to put spinach in our lasagna.

My best friend, Charla Leasure, for serving cake at all my book launch parties. It's not a party without her.

My church, The Journey, for letting me hijack the youth group to be a part of my book trailer.

My agent, Alice Crider, for suggesting I dust off this old manuscript.

My publishing team, including editors John Ashcraft, Andrea Cox, Tami Engle, and Kristen Johnson. All I ever wanted was for a publisher to be as excited about my book as I was. With Ashberry Lane, I got so much more. Because while I was lying in bed too excited to sleep, they were enthusiastically burning the midnight oil to make this happen. Thank you.